'Get yos,
Brad said, with a grin over his shoulder to Sienna and
Jason, as he and Belle headed off.

'Do you have something else planned for tonight?'
Jason asked.

'Well . . .' Sienna gave him one of her slow smiles,
the kind that always made his stomach flip-flop in a
good kind of way. 'Didn't you say your parents had
plans tonight?'

'Yeah. They're off to some business dinner,' Jason
replied.

'And there's *no* possibility Dani is going to miss a
party at Brad's . . .' Sienna continued.

It was true. Jason's younger sister would not let a
party pass her by. It just wasn't possible. He felt
a smile slide across his own face . . .

VAMPIRE BEACH

Don't miss any of the titles in this edgy series:

VAMPIRE BEACH

Hunted

Alex Duval

RED FOX BOOKS

VAMPIRE BEACH: HUNTED
A RED FOX BOOK 978 1 862 30433 8

First published in Great Britain by Red Fox,
an imprint of Random House Children's Books
A Random House Group Company

Red Fox edition published 2008

1 3 5 7 9 10 8 6 4 2

The Random House Group Limited supports the Forest Stewardship Council (FSC), the
leading international forest certification organization. All our titles that are printed on
Greenpeace-approved FSC-certified paper carry the FSC logo. Our paper procurement policy
can be found at www.rbooks.co.uk/environment.
Red Fox Books are published by Random House Children's Books,
61–63 Uxbridge Road, London W5 5SA

www.**kids**at**randomhouse**.co.uk
www.**rbooks**.co.uk

Addresses for companies within The Random House Group Limited can be found at:
www.randomhouse.co.uk/offices.htm

THE RANDOM HOUSE GROUP Limited Reg. No. 954009

A CIP catalogue record for this book is available from the British Library.

Printed and bound in Great Britain by CPI Bookmarque, Croydon, CR0 4TD

To JN, for all the laughs along the way!

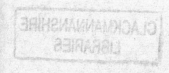

Special thanks to Laura Burns & Melinda Metz

One

The sound of the waves crashing in. The slap of a football being caught in a pair of hands. Girls talking. Guys laughing. Seagulls cawing. A volleyball net flapping in the breeze coming off the ocean. Jason Freeman grinned as he dug his toes deeper into the sun-warmed sand of Surfrider Beach, his eyes closed behind his new Diesel sunglasses. This strip of beach – just your basic paradise – had become his home away from home since he'd moved to Malibu from Michigan at the beginning of his senior year. If someone dropped him on this spot, blindfolded, he'd know it just by the sounds.

That didn't mean he wouldn't miss the visuals, because he definitely would. Jason shoved his sunglasses onto the top of his head, then rolled onto his side, giving himself the perfect view of his favorite Surfrider Beach sight – his girlfriend, Sienna Devereux, in one of her many bathing suits, this one a black bikini with a top that tied in a bow in front. That bow made Jason's fingers itch.

Sienna slid up on one elbow and pulled her big sunglasses down on her nose. She gave him a playful smile, a smile that made him think she could read his mind about that tie.

'You know exactly what I'm thinking, don't you?' Jason asked.

Sienna glanced over to his surfboard, which was jammed in the sand a few feet away. 'That there are some all-time, classic waves out there and you can't let them pass you by?' she asked, widening her eyes with extreme innocence, putting a little surfer-dude spin on her words.

Jason shot a look at the ocean. There *was* some pretty tempting wave action going on out there. He looked back at Sienna. But that bikini bow . . .

How spoiled am I? he thought. *Sitting here trying to decide between two natural wonders: the Malibu coast and my scorching girlfriend. Answer: so insanely spoiled.* Malibu had been very, very good to him. Even if the place was bursting with vampires.

Or maybe *because* it was. There was one vampire who'd definitely made his life more intense and more exciting – Sienna. Being with her made him feel more alive, even though entering her world had nearly made him dead! He'd been attacked by a crazed vampire consumed with bloodlust, and shot with a crossbow by a vampire hunter. And then there was the Aristocratic French vampire who'd been stalking Sienna's sister.

And yet in spite of all the near-death experiences, Jason wouldn't have had his life any other way. Sienna was worth it all. He'd give his life for what they'd already had together, although, ideally, it wouldn't come to that.

'Go ahead. Surf if you want to,' Sienna sighed, settling back to sunbathe.

Jason grinned. 'No way. I'm not surfing. There are much more exciting things to do right here.' He moved closer to Sienna – then reached across her and grabbed the copy of *Cosmo* sticking out of her beach bag. 'I have a lot of reading to catch up on. I haven't even *started* to study the Body Language Decoder.' He opened the magazine and locked his gaze on the page, like it was mesmerizing.

'Decode this,' Sienna said, plucking the magazine out of his hand and tossing it across the sand.

Jason laughed. Then he kissed her. Teasing Sienna was fun, but kissing her was more fun. Way too soon, she pulled back a little and gazed out across the ocean, her expression thoughtful.

'What?' Jason asked, running his fingers down her cheek.

'Just wondering how many days we'll have like this,

with all of us,' she answered. She turned toward the beach where most of the guys were playing football and some of the girls were getting up a volleyball game. Her eyes skipped from face to face, taking in all their friends, pretty much all of them vampires, scattered over 'their' piece of the beach.

Sienna had just brought up the topic that every senior at DeVere High had been avoiding: life after high school. They were just a breath away from graduation. In the fall, they'd be scattered all over the place at different colleges. Forget fall; they'd start splitting up as soon as high school ended. Everybody had summer plans.

'All of us, not that many more times,' Jason admitted. 'But a lot of us, most of the summer. And the two of us, pretty much constantly. Even in the fall. I'm at CalTech. You're at UCLA. We'll practically be room-mates.'

'And together, we're going to own L.A.!' Sienna agreed with a smile, but her dark eyes didn't have all of their usual sparkle as she looked across at her friends.

'So you noticed it too. I can see it in your eyes,' Belle Rémy commented as she grabbed three beers from a nearby cooler and sat down on the other side of Sienna. 'Do you think we should stage an intervention?'

'What?' Sienna asked, staring at her best friend.

'For Adam,' Belle answered. 'Weren't you watching him about to crash and burn with that girl over there?' She jerked her chin toward where Adam Turnball and a short, curvy girl wearing cut-off jeans, a flowered bikini top, and what Jason always thought of as 'smart-chick glasses' – the ones with the black frames – stood loading fish tacos and chips and salsa onto paper plates.

'Well, she's smiling. She doesn't seem to be attempting to back away,' Sienna commented.

'But I heard him use the words Godard, Truffaut and David Lynch in one sentence,' Belle explained. 'And he was using the intense voice. You know, the voice that's one level down from where there's spittle.'

'It's all good,' said Jason. 'Well, not the spittle part. But that girl – yes, that cutie – is here as Adam's date. He invited her here all by himself. Her name's Brianna Graham and Adam met her at a young filmmakers' convention. That means that Godard, Truffaut and David Lynch are actual total turn-ons for her,' Jason explained.

'Huh. Well, good for my little dating protégé.' Belle gave a small nod of approval. 'Maybe someday he'll be able to flirt with someone who *isn't* a film freak.'

Michael Van Dyke intercepted a pass and ran the

football over to the cooler in time to hear Belle's analysis of Adam's love life. 'No girl who looks like that is a freak,' he told her. 'Except for the *good* kind of freak. Know what I'm saying?'

'Belle, are you going to bring us our beer today or what?' Maggie called. Her shortie wetsuit glistened in the sun as she took a practice serve over the volleyball net.

Brad Moreau, Sienna's ex and, kind of surprisingly, the guy who had ended up being one of Jason's closest friends, trotted up to them, breaking the strained silence that had fallen. 'Van Dyke, we're in the middle of a game here,' he said.

'I've officially called a beer break,' Van Dyke replied, hoisting the cooler onto one shoulder and trotting toward the football players.

'Make a stop over here!' Erin shouted from the other side of the volleyball net. 'Belle's deserted us!' Van Dyke obediently veered in her direction.

'Listen up, you guys,' Brad said to Jason, Sienna and Belle. 'Party tonight at my place.'

Sienna raised one eyebrow. 'I thought you were going to cut your parents a break and let them have one out-of-town trip where you *didn't* throw a party,' she said. 'Especially since the trip's for their anniversary and everything.'

'I was,' Brad answered. 'But there's an epidemic in our town and I feel it's my responsibility to do something about it. If I don't provide an outlet for the rampaging "senioritis", some serious damage could be done.'

'Brad's right,' Belle chimed in. 'I definitely won't be held responsible for my actions if I don't have a party to go to tonight. And nobody's parents should go on a special anniversary Caribbean cruise without expecting the offspring to take a little advantage.'

'Besides, this could be our last chance to party *chez Moreau* before we all go off to different colleges and don't see each other again until our ten-year reunion, where we won't be able to think of anything to say to each other,' Brad added.

'Except to talk about how fat and bald the men have gotten and how all the women still look so fabulous,' Belle agreed.

Sienna laughed. 'Wow, I can't wait.'

'So, you're coming tonight, right?' Brad asked.

Sienna shot a glance at Jason. 'We *might*,' she answered.

'What's this "*might*"?' Brad protested. 'I'm telling you—'

'Brad, get over here!' Van Dyke yelled. 'We're combining football with volleyball and a little Frisbee, and we need a rule consult.'

7

'OK!' Brad called back.

'I want in,' Belle said, leaping to her feet. 'Flying folleyball is definitely my game.'

'Get yourselves over to my place tonight. No excuses,' Brad said, with a grin over his shoulder to Sienna and Jason, as he and Belle headed off.

'Do you have something else planned for tonight?' Jason asked.

'Well . . .' Sienna gave him one of her slow smiles, the kind that always made his stomach flip-flop in a good kind of way. 'Didn't you say your parents had plans tonight?'

'Yeah. They're off to some business dinner,' Jason replied.

'And there's *no* possibility Dani is going to miss a party at Brad's . . .' Sienna continued.

That was true. Jason's younger sister would not let a juicy party pass her by. It just wasn't possible. He felt a slow smile slide across his own face. 'So, we could be al—'

Jason didn't have time to finish. Adam slid to a stop in front of them, spraying sand in his wake. 'Should I ask her to the party?' he burst out. 'I think she might actually *like* me. But is it too soon? Because the party is tonight. And we're already doing something today. This, I mean. We're here together. So that would be two events in a row. And isn't that uncool? Am I not supposed to be sort of aloof? Vince Vaughn would definitely tell me not to ask. I don't want to be like the guy in *Swingers* who filled up the answering machine – not that I was going to ask on an answering machine. I was going to ask in person. I'm not a raging doofus, but . . .'

Sienna and Jason looked at each other. Sienna unscrambled the Adam-speak first.

'OK . . . did Brad mention the party in front of Brianna?' she asked.

Adam sucked in a deep breath. 'Yeah.'

'Well, then it would be rude not to ask her if she wants to go,' Sienna decreed. 'Tell her that Brad was definitely inviting everyone.'

'Really?' Adam grinned.

'I don't think at this stage in your dating life you should be playing hard to get,' Jason added.

And Adam was off, sending up another shower of sand.

'What was that *Swingers* answering machine thing he was talking about?' Sienna asked.

'I don't know. Some movie thing. And I never ask him to explain his film references anymore. Ask one movie question and you can't get a word in for at least half an hour,' Jason answered. 'So, before the Adam interruption, we were talking about my house – which is going to be empty tonight, which means we could be alone.'

Sienna snuggled up against him. 'That was what I had planned. Is it uncool of me to tell you that?'

Jason grinned, shook his head and wrapped his arm around her.

'Who knows how many chances we'll have to be alone this summer?' Sienna went on. 'Then when we're in college, we'll both have room-mates . . .' She let her sentence trail off.

She's right, Jason thought. Next year in L.A. was probably going to be great. But could it really compare to what he already had? Was that possible?

'Right now, let's not think about anything but today,' Jason suggested. He pulled Sienna tighter against him, trying to absorb every detail of this moment with her, with their friends, trying to lock in the memory of this little stretch of paradise on earth. Because, in Malibu, things had a way of changing quickly.

Two

'I can't believe I let you drag me away from Sienna for this,' Jason complained to Adam. 'She was wearing the black bikini. Not that it isn't a thrill a minute standing around in the drugstore with you.' He checked his watch. 'You do realize we've been here, in this same aisle, for thirty-two minutes.'

'Thanks for the update,' Adam muttered. He picked up a small orangey-red box, one he'd already picked up about twenty times. He put it down again, and picked up a small neon-green box that he'd also picked up about ten times already.

Jason shook his head. 'I'm still opposed to the Night Lights. One, the name is stupid. It sounds like something that should be in a baby's room. Two, do you really want to be illuminated down there on your first try? I mean, if you know you have the moves, then maybe, but . . .'

'But "Caution Wear" sounds like heavy-duty protection,' Adam commented. 'It doesn't exactly sound fun. Or romantic.' He shot a look down the aisle to make sure it was still clear. 'Can you see it? "Hey, Bree, excuse me a minute, while I slip into the Caution Wear".'

'I don't want to see it. I don't want to *think* about it. Do they sell brainwash in here?' Jason groaned, scrubbing his forehead with both hands.

'I heard this is the brand they use in movies,' Adam said, pointing to another one of the little boxes.

'That's all you'll have to tell Brianna,' Jason joked. 'By the way, Van Dyke was pretty impressed that you scored such a babe,' he added.

'I'm totally impressed with myself,' Adam admitted. 'I mean, she's so out of my league, right? She looks like she could be on one of these boxes' – he tapped the nearest row of condoms – 'and I look like, you know, me.'

'You don't exactly look like you've been raised in the cellar or anything,' Jason told him. 'You shower. You brush your teeth. Belle has stopped you wearing all your truly geek-squad clothing.'

Adam shook his head. 'Still, Brianna and I don't match up on the hot scale, I know. But on the, well, the *soul* scale, we are a perfect match. Two minutes after I met her at the conference, she was telling me how *Inland Empire* had made her swear she was going to shoot in digital her whole life. And just a couple of weeks ago, I wrote this whole blog about deciding that I was never going to shoot on film, that it sucked all the spontaneity and lightness out of a piece. And CGI – well, it can be awesome – but now, I see something with CGI and a little part of my head is saying "fake, fake, fake". Brianna agrees totally. She—'

'OK, OK, I get it. You've found the girl who is worthy of the gift of your precious virginity,' Jason interrupted. 'So pick a box, any box, and go pay.'

Adam shot a look at the counter and groaned. 'I can't.'

'Can we just leave then?' Jason asked. 'Clearly, you aren't going to need any condoms tonight. If you can't even get yourself to buy any, I don't think you're ready for actual sex.'

'Unfair,' Adam answered. But he laughed. 'I'm just waiting for that other cashier to come back. I can't buy condoms from a hot girl. It would be pure bep.'

' "Bep"?'

'Did you even look at the Klingon dictionary I gave you? "Bep" means "agony",' Adam explained. 'And, speaking of bep, couldn't you spare me some, and just give me some of your stash? That way we could leave right now. Or I'll give you money, and you buy me some from the hot cashier. I'm sure you're used to it. I mean, Sienna Devereux walked away from Brad

Moreau for you. And from what I heard from your friend Tyler, it's not like you were hurting for female attention back in Michigan.'

Jason felt his neck and ears turn hot. 'Sienna and I haven't, uh, been together like that,' he admitted.

'Dude! You've put me in a full-on state of shock and awe,' Adam burst out. 'Why not? How could you be in the vicinity of Sienna Devereux for this long without sealing the deal?'

'You're right. Maybe I should have thrown her up against a wall while we were breaking into the lab at her dad's company,' Jason suggested. 'Or, wait, the vault her sister's psycho stalker was holding her hostage in would have been a romantic location. Or the backseat of the vampire hunter's Eldorado. I'm sure he would have let us call a time-out and held off trying to shoot us with his crossbow.'

'You've got a point. These have been strange and dangerous times,' Adam agreed. 'But come on. There wasn't *one* right time? The last few weeks have been pretty tame by DeVere Heights standards.'

Jason decided not to mention that tonight – with his parents and Dani away – could be it, even though that knowledge had been coming to a boil inside him ever since Sienna had told Brad that they might not make his party.

'True. But think about this. Sienna's previous boyfriend was *enhanced*,' he told Adam. 'You've seen what the vampires can do playing football or volleyball. It kind of makes you wonder how good they are at . . . *other* things.'

'Oh, man. I hadn't thought of that – the vampire super-powers and all,' Adam said. 'Wow. I'm glad Brianna's not from V Central.'

Jason grabbed a box of condoms.

'What are you doing?' Adam demanded.

Jason didn't answer. He just strode toward the cute girl behind the counter. When he plunked the box down in front of her, he looked over his shoulder. Adam was further back in the aisle, staring intently at something on the bottom shelf.

'These are for that guy cowering in the feminine hygiene section,' Jason told the cashier, loudly enough for everyone in the store to hear him.

The girl giggled. Adam turned and walked out of the store.

'For that, you are going to suffer a death that will make Willem Dafoe's in *Platoon* look quick and merciful,' Adam announced when Jason joined him outside.

'That movie came out before I was born,' Jason told his friend.

'DVDs have been invented,' Adam reminded him

for the millionth time as he held out his hand for the condoms.

Jason slapped the small paper bag into Adam's hand. 'Good luck,' he said, silently wishing himself the same thing. Tonight really could be *the* night with Sienna.

Jason stared at the blue and red comforter on his bed. It was total guy. Everything in the room was. All the old swimming trophies on his bookshelf. The Active Right Guard Sport deodorant on his dresser. He could at least get rid of that. He opened the top drawer, knocked the deodorant inside, and slammed the drawer shut. That helped . . . almost not at all. His bedroom was still in the negative on the romance-o-meter. Should he take down the poster of—?

The doorbell rang, saving him from turning into a complete nutball. Another few minutes and he'd have been repainting the walls and ripping up the carpet. As he headed to the stairs he heard Danielle saying, 'The place is yours. Kristy and Maria and I are hitting Granita for pizza before we go to Brad's. You be careful. Last time Jason tried to cook something fancy, we almost had to call the fire department.'

'Not true,' Jason called, taking the stairs two at a time.

'Uh-huh. So true,' Dani countered, as she started out the front door. 'He needs supervision in the kitchen,' she warned Sienna. Then she closed the door behind herself, leaving Sienna and Jason alone.

'So you need supervision, huh?' Sienna asked. She walked slowly over to Jason, her long, dark hair falling down her back in a sleek curtain. '*Close* supervision?' she asked, her throaty voice teasing and suggestive at the same time.

'Oh, yeah,' Jason answered. 'Very close.'

Sienna wrapped her arms around his neck. 'I can do that.' And she kissed him, sliding her body tight against his.

'Wait,' she said, stepping away from him. 'What about this fancy food Dani was talking about? Do we need to check on it?'

'It's pretty much on auto-pilot for a while. No worries. I set the timer and everything,' Jason answered.

'I can't believe you're cooking for me,' Sienna told him.

'There's no end to my talents,' Jason laughed. He slipped his fingers under the thin straps of her yellow sundress and started backing toward the couch. He hit the arm of the sofa two steps later. Sienna gave him one of her trademark slow smiles, then put her hands on his chest – and pushed. Not with her full-on vampire strength, but hard enough to send him sprawling onto his back on the sofa cushions – with Sienna on top of him.

Jason slid one hand behind her neck, and pulled her head down to his. Sienna's tongue flicked across his lower lip, a touch that sent shockwaves of sensation slamming through his body.

Forget the beach and the surfing and all that, he thought. This *is the moment I want to hold onto*. He could live in this moment pretty much forever.

Sienna deepened their kiss, her silky hair swirling around both their faces. It smelled like the ocean. The ocean . . . and smoke.

Wait. *Smoke*.

Jason sat up so fast, he almost dumped Sienna onto the floor.

'What?' she demanded.

The smoke detector answered for him, with long, ear-splitting shrieks. Jason bolted for the kitchen, Sienna right behind him. As soon as he whipped open the door, smoke billowed out. He grabbed a dishtowel from the stove door handle, dashed back into the hall-way, and started frantically using it to fan the detector. 'You keep doing this,' he told Sienna, handing over the towel. 'I'll get some windows open.'

'Turn the stove off too,' she suggested.

Jason did that first, dialing the oven down to zero. He didn't even take a peek at his chicken breasts. From the smell, they were already inedible. He raced from window to window, yanking them open as wide as possible. He opened the back door too, then went to check on Sienna. She still hadn't managed to get the smoke detector to stop screaming.

'The thing is supposed to go off at the first whiff of smoke,' he said. 'Whiff.' He jumped up and knocked the plastic cover off, then took out the batteries. The screams subsided. 'Come on. Let's go sit by the pool until the air in here is breathable again.'

Jason ushered Sienna outside and plopped down in a lawn chair. 'Yep, we have the house all to ourselves – the part that hasn't burned down, anyway. Sorry.'

'I was supposed to be supervising,' Sienna reminded him as she sat down on the lounge chair next to him. 'Dani warned me what would happen.'

'So, what do you want to do? We could order in. Or I'll take you anywhere you want to go,' Jason offered.

'With your parents and Dani out, I vote we stay in,' Sienna replied. 'We hardly ever have a place to ourselves.'

'My parents do need to get a life, don't they?' Jason said with a grin. 'Where should we call for food?'

'We're not calling anywhere. This is the best thing

that could have happened. Now we can cook together,' Sienna answered. 'It'll be fun.'

Jason doubted it would be quite as much fun as what they'd been doing on the couch a couple of minutes ago. But they would definitely have a good time. When they were together, they always did. Well, when they weren't right in the middle of life-threatening danger. Although even that wasn't a dead loss with Sienna around.

Sienna checked the oven temperature. 'Three-fifty.' She gave a satisfied nod. Then she set the timer for forty-five minutes. She hadn't allowed Jason to use the stove or even the timer since what they'd started calling '*la fatalité*'.

'Forty-five minutes to make a dessert?' Jason said incredulously.

'It's worth it,' Sienna told him. 'And it'll give us time to clean up this mess.' She walked over to the sink where the charred remains of the first dinner were soaking. 'What did you say this was again?'

'Chicken breasts stuffed with perfection,' Jason answered. 'It was going to be awesome, with feta cheese, and those sun-dried tomatoes you like, and spinach, which I put in for you even though I find it kind of slimy and disgusting.'

'Next time we cook together, we'll make that,' Sienna promised. 'And we'll even leave out the spinach. Now, you start trying to scrub the "perfection" off that pan while I clear the table.' She headed for the dining room. Jason found a Brillo pad under the sink and got to work.

Twenty-five minutes later, the pan had been washed, dried and put away. The dishwasher had been loaded. The sink scrubbed. The floor had even been swept and mopped. Jason and Sienna stood beside the gleaming dining-room table. 'Twenty minutes until dessert,' she said. 'You're going to love the chocolate truffle cake.'

'I can't believe you never told me you could cook,' Jason said.

'All the Devereuxs can cook,' Sienna told him. 'It's a French thing.'

'I don't think I can wait a whole twenty minutes for dessert.'

'You're going to have—' Sienna's words turned into a laugh as Jason wrapped his hands around her waist and swung her up onto the table.

'No.' He shook his head. 'I can't. There's no way I can wait.' He gently lowered her back on the shining wood and climbed up next to her. 'How can I wait when it tastes so good?' He licked a line from her earlobe all the way down her neck. Sienna's laughter turned into a sigh of pleasure that made him crazy.

Jason slid the closest strap on her sundress down, kissed her bare shoulder and . . . heard footsteps! He jerked his head up. *Footsteps!*

He scrambled off the table and swung Sienna down after him, just as his parents walked into the dining room.

'Something smells amazing,' his mother said.

'What are you doing home?' Jason burst out, before he realized that it didn't sound entirely welcoming.

'I couldn't sit there one more second with those arrogant—' Mr Freeman took a deep breath and started again. 'Let's just say that the dinner meeting was unproductive.'

'Doesn't sound like you got any dessert,' Sienna said, throwing Jason a sly smile.

'He hardly got any dinner!' Mrs Freeman answered.

'You two should eat the cake we have in the oven,' Sienna told Jason's parents. 'Just take it out when the timer goes off. It's really good warm.'

'Yeah, dessert's no good if you let it wait,' Jason muttered.

'What about you two?' Jason's mom asked.

'We wanted to head over to Brad's party for a while,' Sienna answered.

Jason raised his eyebrows. Sienna gave him a small, rueful headshake. It was easy for him to interpret. Clearly, they weren't going to get any privacy at the Freeman house that night, so they might as well hit the party.

'You know, one of the last parties before everyone starts going away for the summer, then college,' Sienna added.

'Don't even mention college,' Mr Freeman said. 'This one's mother isn't ready for him to fly the nest.'

'Well, right now, I'm only going a few houses away,' Jason said. 'Enjoy the dessert.'

Somebody should, he thought.

Three

Jason and Sienna turned her Spider over to the valet. Sometimes Jason still had a hard time wrapping his head around the fact that just your basic DeVere Heights high school parties had valet parking. He wondered if there'd always be a little part of him that remained a guy from one of the flyover states.

Mingled cheers and groans came from one side of the Moreaus' Spanish-style mansion as the two of them headed up to the house, hand-in-hand.

'Want to go see whatever that's about?' Sienna asked Jason.

'Why not?' he replied and they veered toward the sound, circling around to the side of the house where Brad had recently convinced his parents to install a regulation-size b-ball court.

'Should have known,' Sienna said, as they spotted Brad and Van Dyke in what looked like a to-the-death game of one-on-one, the crowd about evenly divided between who they were cheering for. 'Those guys. On the first day of kindergarten, Brad was so determined to prove he could go down the slide more times than Van Dyke, he made himself puke. They've been going at it ever since.'

'Are they even going to survive at different schools next year?' Jason watched as Van Dyke casually took a three-point shot from the back of the court – and got nothing but net.

'They'll have to text each other their swimming times and test scores just to function,' Sienna predicted. The guy next to Jason – a junior – let out an amazed cry as Brad raced down the court and hurled the ball at the backboard when he was a little more than halfway down. He leapt into the air, flying up in time to smash the ball down into the net on the rebound.

Sienna frowned. 'Not subtle,' she said softly. It was true that neither Brad nor Van Dyke were giving exactly regular human performances on the court. More like Michael Jordan versus Shaq kind of stuff, only without being six and a half feet tall.

When Van Dyke actually dunked the ball by jumping up to the hoop and swinging from it, Sienna let go of Jason's hand.

'Enough.' Sienna pushed her way courtside, Jason right beside her. 'Brad, you're out of Absolut!' she called.

'Time!' Brad yelled to Van Dyke.

'You couldn't wait until I whipped Van Dyke's butt to tell me that?' Brad asked Sienna.

'She's doing you a favor,' Van Dyke shot back, winking at a ga-ga soon-to-be-senior girl. 'She could tell you needed to catch your breath.'

Sienna moved in close to Brad. 'What I could tell is that you and your friend over there were showing off more than your basketball skills,' she said, quietly enough so that only Brad and Jason could hear. 'Take it down a notch, OK, before people notice that those moves you're throwing down are just too good!'

Brad shoved his fingers through his sweat-soaked hair. 'Got it.' He turned toward the crowd. 'This guy's no challenge for me. Why don't we get a real game going? Who else wants to play?' he asked, shooting Van Dyke a pointed look. Van Dyke gave a small nod back: he'd got the message.

'Want to play?' Sienna asked Jason.

'I think I want to see what Dani's up to,' Jason replied.

'Next year she'll be going to parties all alone without a big brother to protect her,' Sienna reminded him.

'I know. That's why I want to make sure she's learnt how not to be stupid while I'm still around,' he answered. 'And I might see if Adam made it.'

'I think I'll look around for Belle and Erin.' Sienna gave him a long kiss. 'That's to make sure you don't forget me until we find each other.'

'As if.' Jason wandered around to the lagoon-shaped pool in the back of the house. Aaron Harberts, one of the guys on the swim team who wasn't vampirically enhanced, floated in the center, resting on a puffy plastic lounge chair, with a drink in both of the cup holders. A game of Marco Polo where everybody seemed to have their eyes closed – and to be doing a lot of friendly groping – was going on around him.

'Freeman, do you know where I can get a pig?' Harberts called out, wandering over to Jason.

'A pig?' Jason repeated. 'A live pig?'

'No. Dead.' Harberts sounded a little offended. 'But a whole one. I want to roast it. Brad said I could dig a pit over by the fruit trees. They're barbecuing hot dogs and stuff at the bonfire down on the beach. But a roast pig. Wouldn't that taste good right about now?' he asked.

There's a bonfire, a barbecue and bikini-clad chiquitas – the whole deal, Jason thought. *Just the way Brad promised there would be at that first party he invited me to my first week at school. Who needs a pig?*

'How much and what have you ingested?' Jason asked. Then he looked at the blissed-out expression on his friend's face and guessed that a vampire had been feeding on Harberts's blood. Being fed on by a vampire always led to a woozy, euphoric state, and Harberts was definitely in that place.

'I don't know,' Harberts said cheerily. 'But do you know about the pig?'

'Sorry. Nope,' Jason told him.

'That's OK,' Harberts answered with a beatific grin. 'I love you, man. You know that, right?'

'I do,' Jason assured him. Yeah, Harberts had definitely made a blood donation. He'd never told Jason he loved him before. Jason gave his friend a wave, then turned toward the French doors leading into the house. He followed the hard *click-clack* sound to the pool room. His little sister was a complete pool shark and he thought she might be there. But she was giving the suckers a break that night.

Jason joined a darts game featuring the desecrated yearbook photos of some of the most-hated DeVere teachers before checking out the kitchen, where he finally got himself some dessert – although not the one he'd wanted. Dani was holding court in one corner, leading a discussion of how she and the girls surrounding her were going to make this year's Homecoming legendary. It was clear that Dani was going to be one of *the* seniors when the new school year started in the fall. Not that Jason had ever expected anything less.

She's going to do fine without me, he decided. Weirdly, the thought made him feel a tiny bit sad. He grabbed himself a beer from the ice-filled garbage can and wandered into the living room. Adam sat by himself on one end of the half-moon-shaped burgundy sofa, knocking and slapping the glass coffee table rhythmically with his hand. Jason dropped down beside him. 'You really know how to party!'

'I'm working on my new script,' Adam explained. 'Butthead,' he added with a smile. 'Brianna helped me figure out the part I was stuck on. She reminded me of the way they used Morse code in *Independence Day* and suggested I use it in my script. Of course, I'll use it in a much more inventive way. That movie sucked.'

'Of course,' Jason said, mock-solemn as Adam started up his slapping and knocking again. 'So that's what that is?' he asked, nodding at Adam's hand. 'Morse code? I don't know how it works.'

'Yeah. It's basically a binary system, but not exactly, because the length of the pauses between the two sounds are part of the code,' Adam explained.

'I'm . . . not following you,' Jason said.

'There are two sounds in Morse, a long one and a short one. I'm using the slap for long and the knock for short. Each letter in the alphabet is represented by a sequence of slaps and knocks. For example, here's SOS.' Adam knocked on the table three times, slapped three times, then knocked three times again. 'It totally solves the scene I was stuck on. My girlfriend is a genius.'

'Your girlfriend, huh?' Jason asked.

'Well, OK, she's not *technically* my girlfriend, I guess. Whatever it takes to make someone technically your girlfriend,' Adam admitted. 'But obviously I want her to be. I've never had the kind of conversations with anybody that I've had with Brianna. Seriously, I know you think I was exaggerating, but she's a genius. And she gets all my movie references. I said she's a genius, right? And her hair smells really good. I don't know what it smells of, exactly, but it's good. And she makes me laugh. Usually, I'm the guy who makes other people laugh, right?'

'Even when you're not trying,' Jason agreed.

Adam kept right on talking. 'But Brianna cracks me up all the time. And she's *happy*. She's just this happy person. And—'

'I hate to interrupt this conversation,' a girl said from behind them.

Jason turned around and saw Brianna leaning over the sofa's high back, grinning down at them. 'Especially because it was all about me,' she added.

Adam flushed as Brianna walked around and sat down on the arm of the sofa next to him. *I'd probably have turned red if Sienna had heard me gushing about her a couple days after we met*, Jason thought.

At least Brianna was being cool about it. She turned to Jason, giving Adam a chance to recover himself. 'Where can I get one of those?' she asked, nodding at his beer. 'I know there's a massive bar over by the fireplace, but it seems to be mostly for mixed drinks.'

'In the kitchen,' Jason told her. 'Down that hall to the right. There's a big garbage can full of them by the door.'

Brianna laughed. 'I'm glad that some things stay the same. I was starting to feel like I'd wandered into an episode of *My Super Sweet Sixteen* or something. Not that anyone here is that obnoxious. Just that' – she lowered her voice – 'rich.'

'You know I'm not, right?' Adam managed to say.

'Dang! You mean you're not going to finance my first film if I sleep with you?' Brianna teased, standing up. 'I'm going to get that beer and see what other trouble I can get into. I'll be back.'

'That was humiliating,' Adam muttered as soon as Brianna was out of earshot.

'Don't worry about it,' Jason told him. 'Come on, what girl doesn't want to hear that a guy she likes thinks she's great?'

'You think she likes me?' Adam asked.

'She's here. She was at the beach this afternoon hanging with you,' Jason pointed out.

'But do you think she—?'

'Zach's coming over to talk to us,' Jason interrupted. The event was interruption-worthy. Zach Lafrenière didn't usually approach people. People usually came to him. Charisma, Jason's mom would call it. Mojo, Dani would say. Whatever you called it, it was part of what had got Zach on the DeVere Heights Vampire Council when he was still in high school. The youngest member ever.

'Greetings.' Zach set a bottle of wine and three goblets on the coffee table and sat down on the love seat across from Jason and Adam. A couple of people glanced their way. Jason got the feeling they'd like to come over, but Zach was putting out the vibe that he wanted privacy. He pulled a corkscrew out of one of the front pockets of his white linen shirt and opened the wine, then began to pour.

Under the soft party lights, the deep-red wine looked liked it had been made from liquefied rubies. It was almost transfixing.

'You need to try this. It's from my family vineyard. You can't buy it commercially,' Zach told them. There was something different about him. It took Jason a moment to realize that he wasn't wearing his shades. Zach almost always kept his sunglasses on. It was as if he liked having a barrier between him and the world. But tonight he looked from Jason to Adam with his eyes unshielded. They were such a dark brown it was difficult to tell the irises from the pupils.

'It's made completely organically,' Zach continued. 'The plough is even pulled by a winch, so the heavy machinery doesn't pack down the earth.' He handed Jason one of the goblets, then passed one to Adam. The stem of the glass felt faintly warm under Jason's fingers.

'To friendship.' Zach clinked Jason's glass, then Adam's.

I guess even Zach isn't immune from a little end-of-high-school sentimentality, Jason thought.

'You've both been good friends to us,' Zach added.

Now Jason got it. This wasn't just about the end of senior year. This was about appreciation. This was about Zach wanting them to know that he appreciated their help with vampire crises past, and wished them well in the future.

Jason met Zach's gaze and gave a small nod, then took a sip of the wine. It was rich and not too sweet. 'It's good,' Jason said, hoping Zach would get that he was talking about more than the wine. 'Awesome.'

'Truly,' Adam added.

Jason figured that this was about as much of a 'moment' as any of them could take. 'So where are you heading in the fall?' he asked Zach.

'D.C.'

Did that mean a college in the D.C. area? Or . . .? Jason waited for more info, but Zach just took another sip of wine. The guy was back to his usual enigmatic self. He never gave away much. Tonight's exchange with the wine had probably been one of their longer conversations.

'I'm going to—' Jason began.

'CalTech,' Zach finished for him.

Jason and Adam exchanged a look. Zach always seemed to know everything. He probably knew where the two of them were going to be going to college before either of them had even sent in their applications. It was just part of what made Zach Lafrenière Zach Lafrenière.

Jason sat in silence for a while, thinking about what a wild ride it had been since he'd found out the dangerous secret that all the most popular kids at DeVere Heights High shared.

'Eat a pickle,' Van Dyke demanded, yanking Jason away from his thoughts. 'You too, Turnball.' He thrust a pickle jar toward them.

'I'm not eating a pickle,' Jason answered. 'I'm drinking wine, and I just had a beer.'

'Me too,' Adam said.

'I need somebody to eat these pickles,' Van Dyke yelled to the room at large. 'I'm making a batch of witch doctors and I need the juice.'

'Witch doctors?' Jason asked.

'Every kind of alcohol available mixed with the juice of the pickle,' Adam explained.

Zach got to his feet. 'This will require supervision. I don't want to have to drive anyone to the hospital.' He followed Van Dyke over to the bar where a crowd was already forming.

'I think the party has just made the jump to warp speed,' Adam commented.

A few hours later, the party had wound down to whatever was the lowest speed. Not that Brad and Van Dyke had noticed this. They were back on the basketball court, and back in the competitive zone again, as captains of the teams in a three-on-three. Jason, supposedly on Brad's team, had not seen much of the ball. And since Brad didn't look like passing the ball to him – or anyone else – any time this year, Jason was enjoying the warm breeze, the stars, the quiet happiness of being at the tail end of the party with just his closest friends.

Jason noticed that Adam had finally finished 'saying' goodbye to Brianna, so he ducked off the court – probably unnoticed – and headed over to his friend.

'That lipstick's a good color on you,' Jason joked.

Adam wiped his mouth with a grin.

'So I'm guessing you and Bree had a good time,' Sienna commented as she, Maggie and Belle – the other supposed team members – came over to join them.

'Yeah,' Adam said, blushing a little. 'She had to take off, though. She's helping a friend on a shoot at four a.m. tomorrow.'

'I got a chance to talk to her, and I've decided to give her my stamp of approval,' Belle told him. 'I'm proud of you.'

'Way to go, Van Dyke!' Maggie shouted as Van Dyke dunked the ball and swung from the rim.

Jason noticed that they'd really kicked the play into high gear now that Brianna had left. She had been the last human – well, the last *uninitiated* human – at the party.

'Are those two ever going to give it up?' Sienna asked, watching Brad grab the basketball. 'Do they really care so much who is the Supreme Sports Champion of DeVere High?'

'I guess so,' Belle said as Brad bounded toward the

opposite basket, dribbling the ball, then leapt into the air, did a triple flip, and slammed the ball home on his way back to the ground.

'Traveling!' Jason called out, rolling his hands in a circle. 'I did not see any dribbling going on during your final approach to the basket.'

'Yeah, no points for that one. The ball goes back to Van Dyke,' Maggie agreed.

'How was it traveling if my feet weren't on the ground?' Brad protested. 'I didn't take any steps.'

'Oh, shit!' Adam muttered.

Jason followed his gaze and saw Brianna a few feet away, staring at the basketball court.

'Oh, shit,' Jason repeated. Had she seen the vampires acting like . . . vampires?

Four

Jason felt Sienna tense beside him. He knew she was thinking exactly the same thing he was. Had Brianna seen enough to realize that Brad couldn't possibly be human?

'Wow!' Brianna said, her voice coming out choked. 'Does that guy do gymnastics?'

Belle let out a burst of hysterical laughter.

Adam said, 'Yeah, you know these rich kids. Their parents start them with the lessons almost at birth. Me, I'm lucky my dad came up with enough cash for a Happy Meal once in a while.'

'Poor deprived Malibu child,' Maggie cooed.

'It's true about Brad, though,' Jason added. 'He won his first gymnastics trophy when he was . . . What was it, Brad? Four?' he called.

'Three and a half,' Brad answered, strolling over to the group, Van Dyke at his side.

'Most Improved Tiny Tumbler,' Van Dyke told Brianna. 'His mom still has the trophy.'

'No, Most Improved was you,' Brad reminded him. 'I got Terrific Tiny Tumbler. Van Dyke got his award for finally mastering the somersault. It took him a whole year, but he stuck with it.'

'I can still hardly do a somersault,' Brianna confessed. 'I'm not exactly the athletic type. Miniature golf is the only sport I excel in. That's why I'm making Adam take me on Saturday.'

'Did you leave something in the house?' Brad asked, sounding like a concerned host, and not at all like he was freaked and wanted her gone.

'Yeah. My jacket. I'm pretty sure I left it in the kitchen,' Brianna said.

'I'll go with you and check,' Adam told her, and they headed off. As soon as they were out of sight, everybody dropped their fake smiles.

'Do you think she bought the gymnastics thing?' Van Dyke's voice was low and urgent.

'I think so,' Sienna answered. 'She's the one who came up with it.'

'I thought everyone was gone. Everybody . . . you know.' Brad shook his head, clearly annoyed with himself.

'We all did,' Van Dyke said. 'I was screwing around as much as you. Anyway, no harm, no foul, right?'

'Right,' Maggie answered.

'You ready to head off?' Jason asked Sienna. The party definitely felt done now.

She nodded.

'Your parents didn't by any chance have a late-night appointment that would leave your house empty, did they?' he asked as they headed to her car.

'We're out of luck for tonight,' she answered, wrapping her arm around his waist. 'But dessert is definitely on the menu sometime soon.'

'You're lucky I'm such a good friend,' Jason told Adam quietly as they slowly trailed Brianna and Sienna to the third hole of the Sunshine Castle Miniature Golf course on Saturday afternoon. 'There are very few people I would play putt-putt golf for.'

'I'm with you, bro. If I wanted to induce a bout of narcolepsy, this is where I'd come,' Adam answered. 'Except, today, Brianna's with me and she loves this place. And I owe her one because she promised to go see a screening of *A Clockwork Orange* with me tonight, even though she hates violent movies. Speaking of the blood and gore, wanna watch *Reservoir Dogs* with me after school on Monday? I don't suppose you've seen it, since it didn't come out yesterday, but I know you'll dig it. And we need some male bonding time.'

'Sure,' Jason said. 'But you have to provide snacks.

Lots of snacks. Because now you owe *me*.' He nodded his head in the direction of a smiling lavender and yellow dragon off in the distance at the thirteenth hole. 'This place is a candy-colored nightmare.'

'We're up, guys,' Sienna called, waving them forward. 'Jason, do you think you could help me line up my shot?' she asked, in complete flirt mode.

'What was I complaining about again?' Jason asked Adam.

'Dude, I don't know,' Adam answered as they hurried to join the girls.

'Thanks for doing this,' Jason said in Sienna's ear as he wrapped his arms around her and placed his hands over hers on the golf club. 'I know it's not your thing.'

'Who says it's not?' she whispered back, giving Jason a flirtatious smile.

Then it was Jason's shot. He focused on trying to get his orange golf ball over the little bridge and through the spinning blades of the windmill.

'Yes! The Force is certainly with *you* today, Jason,' Brianna cried. 'I think you sent that ball into warp speed!'

Adam laughed. 'I think you mean *light*speed,' he said.

'D'oh!' Brianna smacked her forehead with her hand.

'What are you guys talking about?' Sienna asked.

' "Warp speed" is *Star Trek*. But the "Force" is *Star*

Wars,' Adam explained. 'Therefore, nobody using the Force could ever, under any circumstances, send anything into warp speed – without the universe of cinema imploding.'

Jason sank the ball and Bree clapped.

'One under par,' Adam announced. 'You keep this up, you might just win.'

'Do we eat crap food here or go out to a real place?' Jason asked when they'd finished the eighteenth hole. He'd come in with the lowest score, and the others had decided that, since he'd had the pleasure of beating them, he could buy them lunch.

'Oooh, delicious, delicious crap food please,' Brianna cried, clasping her hands together in front of her.

'This is my kind of girl,' Jason said.

'Mine too,' Adam agreed as they walked to the outdoor food court between the mini-golf and the bumper boats. 'Except for that.' He gestured to the slogan on Brianna's T-shirt, which read 'Independent Filmmakers Do It Alone'.

Brianna and Sienna exchanged a you-know-boys look and laughed.

'Well, you're an independent filmmaker too, Adam,' Brianna told him. 'So what happens when two independent filmmakers get together? Do they still do it alone? Or does some kind of collaboration take place?'

'I'm very interested in collaboration,' Adam said weakly. He was clearly almost too overwhelmed by the collaboration idea for speech.

'We'll let them discuss and save a table while we go select an assortment of crap,' Sienna suggested to Jason. 'Any requests?'

'I like the greasy-salty kind especially,' Brianna said.

'They're very cute together,' Sienna commented as she and Jason got in line at the kiosk that seemed to have the highest grease and salt quotient.

'As cute as us?' Jason asked.

'No one is as cute as us,' Sienna countered.

Jason grinned. 'Did you notice Adam's reaction when he caught Brianna mixing up *Star Wars* and *Star Trek*?' he asked. 'He laughed. *Laughed!* If I'd done that, I would have been forced to watch every *Star Wars* and *Star Trek* movie before Adam would allow me to resume our friendship. And, only then, after I passed a quiz,' Jason said.

'Adam can be a little extreme,' Sienna commented.

'He's a film geek. It's his nature,' Jason said. 'The weird thing is, Brianna's a film geek too. By their standards, that was a rookie mistake to make.'

'No one can know every movie fact by heart,' Sienna answered. 'Not even Adam.'

'We're not talking just any movie fact. We're talking—'

Sienna cracked up.

'What?' Jason asked.

'Adam's rubbing off on you,' Sienna told him. 'You're becoming a geek, too!'

'No way,' Jason shot back.

'You were a breath away from giving me a lecture on movie facts. Admit it.' Sienna gave him a gentle poke in the stomach. 'I don't know if I can start college with a geek boyfriend.'

'I was just trying to explain why it was weird that Bree made that goof.' A sudden thought made Jason grin. 'Maybe Adam's taste is a little too *popular* for Bree. Maybe she only likes "films". Not movies. You know, I bet she only watches things with subtitles, or interesting lighting effects, or whatever. Maybe she hasn't even seen all the *Star Wars* movies!' he exclaimed.

'You don't have to sound so happy about it,' Sienna told him.

'I just love the idea of their first fight being about *Adam's* bad taste in movies. It's funny to me. All I hear from him is how he can't believe I haven't seen this or that movie. Now Brianna will be telling him she can't believe he actually likes, I don't know, *The Matrix*. Although she has seen *Independence Day*, but maybe that was a fluke. I'm hoping.'

Sienna shook her head at him. 'You're evil.'

'No, I'm not,' Jason protested. 'I don't want them to break up over it or anything. I just like the idea of Adam being on the other side of an Adam-style movie tirade.'

'Evil,' Sienna repeated, laughing.

'How was the mini-golf?' Dani asked when Jason walked into the kitchen.

'I won,' he told her.

She made an exaggerated I'm-impressed face.

'What's the deal here, Mom?' Jason asked. His mother was sitting at the table, flipping through a copy of O magazine. 'No cookies, no brownies, no baked goodies of any kind? I thought you were on a campaign to remind me how good life at home is, so that I'm sure to come back from college every weekend.'

'Mom got good news. It made her forget all about you and your nest-leaving,' Danielle explained.

Jason sat down in the empty chair between his mother and his sister. 'What kind of news?'

'I finally heard from your Aunt Bianca,' Mrs

Freeman exclaimed, beaming. 'You know how worried I've been. I haven't heard from her in months. She hasn't returned a single call.'

'What did she say?' Jason asked, careful not to look at his sister. His mother was almost psychic about reading her kids' expressions. If he glanced at Dani, he was afraid his mother might figure out that they had a secret and try to figure out what it was. And it was something that neither of them ever wanted her to know: her sister, their aunt Bianca, was a vampire. She'd been turned into a vampire by her vampire husband Stefan before he'd died. She'd even inherited his place on the Vampire High Council.

But Stefan hadn't known that Bianca's human genetic make-up meant that she couldn't tolerate becoming a vampire. She had succumbed to transformation sickness, and had been slipping deeper and deeper into insanity. The last time Jason had seen her, back in February, she was already seriously unstable. Who knew what she would be like by now?

'She said that she'd been having some health problems, but she'd found an excellent treatment,' Mrs Freeman told him.

'And apparently she said she'll probably be in California soon,' Dani added, shooting Jason a quick glance.

Jason couldn't quite tell if she was worried or excited. Did she believe his aunt had actually found a treatment for the transformation sickness? Was it possible?

Jason doubted it. If there was a treatment, the DeVere Heights Vampire Council would know about it, and he would have heard about it from Sienna. He hadn't heard anything about his aunt from Sienna or Zach, even though the Council was supposed to be trying to keep tabs on Bianca.

'I think I'll go check the guest room. Just in case,' his mother said. 'You know how Bianca loves to pop in unannounced.' She hurried from the room.

'You think she might?' Danielle asked quietly.

'Doubtful,' Jason told her. 'If Bianca showed up in California, the DeVere Heights Vampire Council would probably take her under their protection – by which I mean "get her under their control" – before she made it to our house.' And Jason couldn't help thinking that that was a good thing. His human family just wasn't prepared to handle Bianca's vampire problems.

'Who am I going to talk to about this stuff when you're away at school? What if something, you know, *happens*?' Danielle asked.

'L.A.'s hardly far away,' Jason said. 'A call, and I'm here. And don't think I won't hear about anything I need to hear about when I'm at CalTech.'

'Don't get carried away. It's not like I need you to tell me my skirt is too short or something. Or check up on me at a party – which I know you did at Brad's, so don't deny it.'

'I'm not going to,' Jason answered. 'I'm your big brother. It's what I do.'

'I can take care of myself. I'm only one year younger. Just if anything really weird goes down . . .'

'I'm there,' Jason promised.

His cell phone began to play the Pussycat Dolls' song *I Don't Need a Man*. 'I thought you'd grown out of changing my cell ringer,' he said to Dani.

'For old times' sake,' Dani answered with a cheeky grin. 'I only have you here for a few more months.'

Jason checked the caller ID: Sienna.

'Hey, I was wondering if you could come over,' she said before he could even say hello.

'You miss me already?' he asked.

'Absolutely,' she answered, but he didn't think her voice had quite its usual playfulness.

'Anything wrong?'

'No. I just don't feel like being alone,' she said.

'On my way.' Jason hung up the phone. He could read Sienna as well as she could read him. And she was clearly not telling him everything. Something was very wrong.

Five

Jason reached Sienna's house faster than he should have legally been able to. *Her parents don't know what time you left the house,* he reminded himself when he spotted them coming out of their front door.

'Hi,' he called to them as he climbed out of his VW Karmann Cabriolet. Had Sienna called him because she was about to achieve Empty House? She hadn't said so, but maybe her parents had been in hearing range . . .

'Hello, Jason,' Mrs Devereux said. Her tone snapped Jason out of his Sienna-fuelled fantasy. It wasn't angry or unfriendly, but there was an undercurrent of strain, and her smile seemed forced.

'Do you have more luggage I can help you with?' Jason asked, registering that Mr Devereux was loading a couple of bags into the trunk.

'I've got them, thanks,' Mr Devereux said. He shut the trunk with a quiet click, then opened the passenger door for his wife.

Sienna hurried outside. 'I found your cell,' she told her father, handing it to him.

'Thanks, sweetheart.' Mr Devereux kissed her on the cheek. 'We'll call when we get there. Goodbye, Jason. Sorry to rush off.'

He got behind the wheel of the car. Jason and Sienna watched as it glided down the driveway and into the street.

'What's going on?' Jason asked.

'That's just it. I don't know,' Sienna admitted, her eyes on the spot where the car had disappeared from view. She turned to him. 'Come on, let's go inside.'

Jason followed her into the Devereuxs' elegant living room. 'My father got a call about forty-five minutes ago,' Sienna explained as they sat together on the sofa, 'and all of a sudden, he and my mom were rushing around, packing. All they would tell me is that they needed to go to Chicago on some Council business, and that they shouldn't be gone too long. Not that they could tell me when they'd be back. It was really weird. My parents usually give me loads of information. You know, phone numbers for everyplace they'll be, even though they both have cells, and everything. But not this time . . .' Sienna leant her head against Jason's shoulder. 'I didn't mean to be all dramatic on the phone.'

'You weren't,' Jason reassured her.

'It's just that them being so secretive makes the whole thing a little scary. A couple of years ago they had to go out of town for a big gathering. There was a threat that the head of one of the French families was going to be assassinated. My parents didn't tell me a lot, but they told me the basics,' Sienna continued. 'This time, all they would say was that Zach was staying in town in case any problems came up.'

'Have you talked to him yet?' Jason asked. Zach was absolutely the person he'd want to get the facts from. 'He's in the Council. If anyone would know the real deal, he would.'

'Tried. But he didn't answer,' Sienna said. 'I called everybody else though. Everyone's parents are heading to Chicago. Even Brad's. They're cutting their anniversary cruise short. They wouldn't do that for something minor. So help me brainstorm. What do you think could be up?' She gave a rueful laugh. 'This is how you wanted to spend your Saturday night, right? Sitting around with me, coming up with conspiracy theories.'

'I love coming up with conspiracy theories,' Jason told her. 'It's one of the few times my highly-developed paranoia is an asset.'

'Thanks.' She let out a sigh that seemed to release a

little tension from her body. 'I really didn't want to be alone with all these crazy thoughts running around in my brain. I know my parents wouldn't have left me here by myself if they thought I was in any danger.'

'That's totally true. Maybe there was some kind of accounting scandal. You know, somebody got caught buying five-thousand-dollar shower curtains with Council money or something.' Jason ran his fingers through Sienna's hair.

'Probably. Anything to do with money can make my dad's head go volcanic,' Sienna agreed, sounding a bit more hopeful.

'Or maybe a non-vampire somehow wormed his or her way to the very top of the Council and a tell-all book is about to hit the stores,' Jason suggested.

Sienna smiled a little, but her eyes had a faraway look. He hadn't been able to completely take her mind off the situation. Maybe if he kissed her . . .

What was he thinking? He was here as the supportive boyfriend. He wasn't supposed to be trying to score.

Sienna tilted her face up so she was looking into his eyes. The distracted look was gone. 'Come here,' she said, using one hand to pull his head down to hers. And then, what was there to do but kiss her? And kiss her. And kiss her. And . . . kiss . . . her . . .

Their lips didn't break apart even as Sienna twisted her body and straddled him. He ran his hands under the flowy embroidered top she had on, all the way up her bare back. Completely bare. Some part of his brain registered that she wasn't wearing a bra.

Then Sienna's hands were under his T-shirt, sliding it up, sliding it off, their kiss ending as she pulled back to look at him. She glided the fingers of one hand from his chest to his belly button. His heart slammed into his ribs as her hand moved on down, past the waistband of his jeans – and then they both froze as someone pounded on the front door.

Sienna scrambled off his lap and swept her hair away from her face. Jason pulled on his T-shirt, realized it was on inside out, pulled it off, and put it back on the right way.

'Coming!' Sienna called, rushing for the door. Jason stayed where he was. He needed a minute to compose himself. Yeah, that was a good word for it: 'compose'.

There wasn't much time for composure before Sienna led Zach, Brad and Van Dyke into the living room. Brad and Van Dyke seemed too worked up to notice that they might have been interrupting something between Jason and Sienna. But Zach noticed everything. Jason knew he'd drawn the correct conclusion, even though his expression didn't change.

'Belle, Maggie and Erin are on their way,' Zach announced, taking a seat. 'There are things you all have to know.'

'So you're finally going to tell us what's going on?' Brad burst out.

'Yeah, and I only want to do it once,' Zach answered.

'Anybody want drinks while we wait?' Sienna asked. She rushed out of the room without waiting for an answer. Jason didn't follow her. He figured maybe she needed a little composing time too. When she returned, her hair was a little smoother, and her face wasn't as shiny. She carried a tray of sodas and beers.

'I see Maggie's car pulling up. She was collecting the other two. I'll go let everybody in,' Van Dyke said. A few moments later, the entire group was assembled in the living room.

Brad looked over at Zach. 'The floor is yours,' he said.

'I wanted to tell you why the meeting has been called in Chicago,' Zach told them. 'Not everybody thought you needed to know, but I do. I'm filling in everyone who was left behind in the Heights. This is big . . .'

'Well, what is it?' Belle demanded impatiently.

Jason saw that she looked frightened. *After what happened to Dominic, why wouldn't she be?* he thought.

Belle's boyfriend had been killed by the same vampire hunter who had shot Jason with the crossbow and tried to kill Sienna. Jason figured she probably went into any strange situation expecting the worst.

'Some disturbing things have been happening in New York for a while,' Zach continued. 'Vampires started disappearing, for a night or maybe a weekend. When they returned, they were disorientated. They couldn't remember what had happened to them, and they were physically weak and exhausted. It was almost like they'd been on drinking binges.'

'But a vampire would have to drink a *phenomenal* amount to get *that* effect,' Van Dyke protested. 'I had about eight witch doctors at Brad's party and I was fine.'

'I wouldn't say that,' Brad joked lamely.

'Drinking doesn't seem like a plausible explanation,' Zach agreed. 'But the council hasn't been able to come up with any explanations that *are* plausible, that's the problem . . .'

Jason waited for it. He could tell there was more.

'Lately, in the last month or so, vampires have started disappearing in other parts of the country,' Zach went on.

'Same deal? No memory of what happened?' Erin asked, leaning forward.

Zach gave a brief head shake. 'They didn't come back at all.'

'Shit,' Van Dyke muttered.

'Vampires from all over the country are gathering in Chicago to join forces, combine information and try to figure out what's going on. It's surprising that there isn't more intel already, considering how well-connected we are,' Zach said.

'Have there been any disappearances around here?' Jason queried.

'Not yet,' Zach told him. 'Trust me, the DeVere Heights Council would not have left Malibu if they thought there was any danger here.'

'But *you* do,' Jason pointed out. 'Otherwise, why—'

'I'm just taking precautions,' Zach said, raising a hand to quell any panic from the others. 'That's all.'

'What is it? Is it vampire hunters? Could a group of vampire hunters be working together all over the country?' Belle asked anxiously. Sienna and Erin both moved closer to her.

'Unlikely,' Zach replied. He hesitated, then looked Belle in the eye. 'If you remember, the hunter who came here was happy to leave the bodies behind.'

'And he hunted alone,' Van Dyke added.

'But I suppose it's possible,' Zach finished.

They all sat in silence for a few moments. Jason grabbed a soda just to have something to do.

'Should we arrange a buddy system or something?' Brad suggested finally.

'I don't think we need to go that far,' Zach answered. 'As I said, there haven't been any disappearances in our area.'

'Can I ask a newbie-ish question?' Jason didn't wait for permission. 'You said vampires are disappearing all over. Are there vampires everyplace? In every city in the country?'

'No place is like Malibu, dude,' Van Dyke answered. 'We own this place.'

'Practically,' Brad agreed with a smile.

'Our kind live all over the country. Not in every city, but in many,' Zach explained. 'But the DeVere Heights vampires are from purer bloodlines. That means we're more powerful, physically and politically, than most other American vampires.'

'Got it,' Jason said.

'I want to go back to that buddy system idea,' Belle said, looking around the room. 'I know we can all kick ass and everything, but I really don't want to be alone.'

'You don't have to be,' Sienna said immediately. 'You're spending the night.'

'Sleepover!' Erin called.

'Absolutely. All my girls are staying,' Sienna answered.

Which meant the house was not going to be empty again for a while. Not that Jason was going to complain. He didn't want Belle – or Sienna – to be alone, either.

'And tomorrow afternoon, once you girls roll out of bed, barbecue at my place,' Van Dyke said. 'We may as well all hang together. Just us.' He shot a look at Jason. 'And friends of us, of course.'

'Does that include Adam?' Jason asked.

'Adam definitely qualifies,' Van Dyke decreed. 'He can even bring the hot chick. Who I know has a name,' he told Maggie and the other girls, 'but I don't happen to remember it right now.'

'Brianna,' Sienna informed him.

'Brianna can also come. As long as Brad keeps his gymnastics to a minimum,' Van Dyke added.

'You were—' Brad began, then seemed to give up.

'This will be so fun!' Belle exclaimed. 'We haven't had a slumber party in forever. You can loan me a T-shirt or something to sleep in, right?' she asked Sienna. 'I don't want to bother going home.'

'All of you can borrow whatever you need. None of you are going home. The party starts now,' Sienna told her girlfriends.

'And if there's something you absolutely can't get along without, I'll be your errand boy,' Jason volunteered. 'There's no reason for a mere human to be afraid.'

'Do you have any Cherry Garcia?' Erin asked Sienna. She shook her head.

'Jason, will you go buy us some Cherry Garcia?' Erin begged.

'Sure.' He stood up.

'And some vinegar Pringles?' Belle asked.

'Gross, but sure,' Jason told her.

Brad and Van Dyke snickered. 'Whipped,' Van Dyke mumbled under his breath.

'I want those coconut macadamia cookies. I can't remember what they're called. But Van Dyke knows what the package looks like.' Maggie smiled at her boyfriend. 'I guess he'll have to go with you.'

Brad laughed.

'I don't know what you're laughing for – you're driving,' Van Dyke told Brad.

'Thank you,' Sienna mouthed as Jason and the other guys were pelted with more requests.

'Anytime,' Jason mouthed back.

Six

Jason ran down the steep steps leading to the beach just as the sun was weaving the first threads of pink and gold across the dark cloth of the ocean. It was pretty much only him and his board out there, although he could see one hardcore surfer already in the water, waiting for his ride.

For some reason he'd woken up insanely early for a Sunday morning, and he hadn't been able to fall back asleep. So he'd decided to give it up and get in some work on his frontside roundhouse cutback. He hadn't mastered the move, not by a long shot, and it would take all his focus.

He swam out to the line-up, the spot where the waves started to break, the water chilly even through his wetsuit. The Pacific never got very warm here. But neither did Lake Michigan, and Lake Michigan didn't have waves, so he wasn't complaining.

Jason straddled his board and waited until he saw a wave coming in that he liked. A nice tall one. The roundhouse needed speed, and for speed he needed to start high on the top of the wave. He flattened himself out on his belly and paddled for the shore as fast as he could. He felt the back of his board lift as the sweet wave rose up beneath him.

He popped to his feet, then started down the wave's face. Then before the wave flattened out too much, he started his turn. He leant back a little, but kept his board flat. If he let the board tip, he'd lose momentum. *Wait for it, wait for it,* Jason coached himself. *Now!* He pressed down on his heels and lifted the balls of his feet – and went spinning out. The wave crashed over him, and Jason came up coughing.

He'd broken the number one rule of surfing. He hadn't kept the majority of his body weight over the midpoint of the board. Well, nothing to do but try again.

For the next hour, Jason worked on his turn until his entire body felt battered, and he'd managed to perform the move correctly three times in a row. He'd even managed to touch the water with his inside hand on the last try. That was true style.

Jason decided to quit on that moment of triumph. As he paddled to shore, he spotted Adam on the beach. 'What are you doing here?' Jason asked as he climbed out of the water with his board.

'Thought you might be here,' Adam said. 'I went by your house and saw your car was gone. I'm jonesing for a Rooty Tooty Fresh 'n' Fruity. Shall we hit IHOP?'

'Well, I've already eaten a double helping of the ocean floor,' Jason admitted. 'But I could probably squeeze in a pancake. Hey, did you see my last turn?'

'Yeah. You almost took another spill. Nice recovery,' Adam answered.

'Leaning over and touching the water like that is *style*,' Jason corrected as he toweled off. 'It's flair. It's finesse.'

Adam shrugged. 'Well, it looked like you were about to fall on your butt.'

'Did you talk to Bree about Van Dyke's barbecue?' Jason asked Adam as they started for the steps in the side of the cliff.

'We'll be there,' Adam said. 'I've even got the OK to borrow my dad's car, so I can pick her up. She's at her friend's place in Topanga Canyon, so the Vespa wasn't really an option.'

'Van Dyke is going to be most impressed,' Jason told him.

'Well, I live to impress Van Dyke,' Adam shot back.

'Thanks, this looks great!' Jason said, as Van Dyke

handed him a plate of grilled steak, corn on the cob and baked beans, later that day.

'Jason's easily impressed by cooking skills,' Sienna laughed from the deck chair next to his. 'He's still working on Egg Boiling 101.'

Van Dyke grabbed another deck chair and dragged it up next to theirs. 'I'm not surprised. He's backward in many areas. I was just getting him up to speed as a member of the relay team, and now school is almost over.' He shook his head sadly.

I'm going to miss this clown, Jason thought. He didn't hang out with Van Dyke except as part of the bigger group, but Van Dyke always made any event more entertaining. 'What are you doing this summer?' Jason couldn't believe he'd never asked.

'No big plans. Enjoy the Malibu summer,' Van Dyke said with a shrug. 'Get ready to leave for Harvard.'

Jason raised his eyebrows. 'Harvard? You going to swim for them?'

'Pre-law.'

Jason frowned. 'Wow! I'm impressed. I didn't even know you had an interest in law.'

'Had young Mr Freeman paid attention to anything other than the lovely Ms Devereux all year, he might have acquired a few interesting facts about his other class-mates,' Van Dyke said with a grin, giving Jason a friendly slap on the shoulder. Jason was pretty sure it would leave a bruise.

'I've—' Jason began to protest.

I know. You've had a few other—' Van Dyke began, but he was interrupted by the ring of his cell. 'Talk to me,' he said, flipping it open. He listened for a moment, his expression turning serious. 'I'm leaving now.' He snapped the phone shut. 'That was Maggie.'

'Where is she?' Sienna asked. 'She said she was only going home to change her clothes.'

'While she was in the house someone slashed her tires,' Van Dyke said.

'What?' Belle exclaimed, an ear of corn poised halfway to her mouth.

'I didn't even know they tolerated that kind of petty crime in DeVere Heights,' Jason commented. 'I thought this was a strictly white-collar crime zone.'

Brad barked out a laugh. 'Maybe the little juniors are feeling very mature and bad ass now that the school is about to become theirs, and one of them did it.'

Van Dyke shrugged. 'I'm going to go pick her up,' he said. 'One of you watch the grill. Get whatever you want from the fridge.' He hurried away around the side of the house.

Zach tossed another steak on the fire. Erin turned the music up a little louder.

'Aren't Adam and Brianna supposed to be here too?' she asked Jason a little later.

'I saw Adam this morning and he said they would be,' Jason told her. 'And you know how Adam hates to miss free food.'

'He and Brianna probably wanted to get in a little alone time first,' Sienna said. 'They're a new couple, remember.'

As if Jason was past wanting to get in a little alone time with her!

'Does anyone know what we're doing for senior cut day?' Belle asked. 'Last year the seniors skipped school and went to the Santa Monica pier. But that's too ordinary.' She dipped a foot into the pool.

'I thought every day was senior cut day now anyway,' Brad joked.

'Not if you have Mr Tomlinson,' Sienna said. 'He announced to all his classes that if anyone is absent without a doctor's note – a doctor's, not just a parent's – he will personally write to the college where you've been accepted and tell them to reconsider because you lack the proper seriousness.'

'Ed Gerner's mom's a doctor. He'll sell you a piece of her office stationery for a hundred bucks,' Zach threw out.

'You know his mom's a cosmetic surgeon, right?'

Erin asked. 'So you guys might want to come up with a plan B.'

'Maybe we could go on a tour of the stars' homes for cut day,' Belle suggested. 'I've lived practically on top of Hollywood my whole life and I've never done that.'

'Maybe because it's so incredibly tacky?' Erin asked.

'That's why it would be fun,' Belle told her.

Everyone threw out more possibilities for cut day, until Belle announced she was frying in the sun. 'I'm going in the pool. I don't care if I don't have my bathing suit.'

Brad looked intrigued. Jason tried not to look intrigued. Belle laughed as she jumped into the pool with all her clothes on.

'I'm going in too!' Erin leapt into the pool without even taking off her jeweled flip-flops.

Jason stood up and grinned at Sienna. She grinned back and took a step toward the pool. Then her cell rang. She pulled it out of her purse and answered, then frowned as she listened.

'He definitely already left, Maggie,' Jason heard her say. 'He should be there. Call me as soon as he shows up, OK?'

'Van Dyke's not at Maggie's yet?' Jason asked as Sienna hung up. Every eye was on Sienna as she shook her head.

'Maggie lives in the Heights,' Zach said. 'Five minutes away.'

Jason nodded as everyone exchanged worried glances. They all knew that Van Dyke should have been there *and* back, already.

Seven

Belle climbed out of the pool and wrapped herself in a beach towel. The afternoon sun was hot, but Jason could see that she was shivering. She was still so on edge after Dominic's death.

'Call Van Dyke,' Jason suggested.

Sienna nodded and punched Van Dyke's speed dial number on her cell. 'His voice mail's picking up,' she told the group. 'Hey, it's Sienna,' she said into the phone. 'Maggie's wondering where you are, and so are we. Call us.' Slowly, she clicked the phone shut.

'That's it. I'm going to look for him,' Brad announced. Jason stood up. 'I'll go with you.'

'Me too,' Sienna said.

'No,' Jason told her. She stared at him. 'Some people need to be here in case he shows up,' he explained. Which was a reason, just not *the* reason. He knew Sienna could handle herself in threatening situations. He'd seen her do it. He even knew that she was stronger than he was, stronger and faster. But he didn't want her out there when who knew what was going on. The only thing they were sure of was that vampires were disappearing. Maybe whatever had happened to Van Dyke had no connection to the disappearances. But if it did, Jason was in less danger than Sienna was. So he wanted her here, with Zach and the others. This was the safest place she could be.

'Please,' he said softly.

'OK,' Sienna agreed. 'But be careful. Remember you're only human.'

Jason nodded, then he and Brad raced out to Brad's car. Brad drove to Maggie's slowly, so they could both look for any sign of Van Dyke. They didn't see his car or any indication of an accident.

Maggie burst out onto the driveway the instant they pulled up. 'Where is he?'

'We're not sure, Mags,' Brad told her. 'Maybe he decided to stop on the way for something? More ice or paper towels?' He gave a helpless shrug.

'What if that's not what's happened?' she snapped.

'We don't know what's happened,' Jason said firmly. 'Let's head back to his house. Does he always take the same route over here?'

Maggie rattled off the same streets they'd used to come by. There was no sign of Van Dyke on the way back.

'Did he call?' Brad asked, when they joined the others who were now gathered in the living room of Van Dyke's house.

'No,' Zach said simply.

'So what do we do now?' Sienna asked.

Before anyone could answer, the doorbell rang.

'Maybe it's him!' Maggie exclaimed, rushing to answer it.

The others waited in silence. Nobody bothered to point out that Van Dyke wouldn't ring his own doorbell.

'It's Adam and Brianna,' Maggie announced, leading them into the living room. Her voice was strained.

Jason got it. He didn't particularly want an outsider here right now, either. They were all way too worried about Van Dyke to bother pretending they weren't vampires in front of Brianna.

'Listen, Turnball. Something came up unexpectedly that Van Dyke had to deal with,' Zach told Adam. 'I'm sorry, but I think you should take Brianna home now.'

Adam immediately seemed to take in what category of unexpected something they were dealing with. 'All right,' he answered. 'Is there anything I can do?' he asked. 'Maybe there's an errand I can run on my way back home? Or I could drop back by here and check in to see if you need anything?'

'It's under control,' Zach said pleasantly, but firmly.

'All right,' Adam repeated. 'We'll get going.'

'I hope everything's OK. Um, tell Van Dyke thanks for inviting me,' Brianna told the group. Then she turned and followed Adam out of the room.

'So what do we do?' Sienna asked again when Adam and Brianna had pulled out of the driveway.

'Is there any way to get in touch with our parents?' Erin asked.

Zach shook his head. 'The meeting is being held in an area that doesn't have cell phone service or land lines. But this is something we should be able to handle ourselves.'

'That's not an answer,' Erin said impatiently.

'It's all the answer I have for now,' Zach told her. 'There's no point in doing anything without information. For now, we go on as normal. That means school tomorrow. I'll get in touch with my sources and see what I can find out.'

'That's it? We just go to school and sit on our butts?' Brad demanded, his face twisted with anger.

'For now, yes,' Zach replied, his voice even and unemotional. It was clear from his tone that the discussion was over.

'I'm at least going to drive around town and see if I spot him anywhere,' Brad said.

'I'll go with you,' Maggie insisted.

'If you do see any sign of him, call me. I don't want either of you to take any action without my approval,' Zach told them.

Brad hesitated a fraction of a second, then nodded.

'Bring Maggie back to my place when you're done, OK?' Sienna asked.

'OK,' Brad said.

Sienna glanced from Belle to Erin. 'I guess we should all go back to my house. Will you take us, Jason?'

'Of course. Come on.'

'I'm going to stay here. If he shows up, I'll call all of you,' Zach told them as they trooped to the front door.

The drive to Sienna's only took a few minutes. 'Will you three be OK or do you want me to stay?' Jason asked.

'I think I want to go back to bed,' Belle said with a wide yawn.

'We stayed up pretty late last night,' Sienna explained. 'I think we'll probably all go to sleep. You should just go home.' She leant over and gave him a kiss that landed on the corner of his mouth. 'I'll see you at school.'

Jason watched until Sienna, Erin and Belle were safely inside. He thought about staying parked in the driveway, keeping guard. But Zach wanted them to act normally, and that wasn't normal, so he started home.

As he made a left turn, he felt his shoulder twinge, although the crossbow wound there had completely healed. Psychosomatic, he decided. The disappearing vampires had gotten him thinking about vampire hunters.

It's true that Tamburo – the vampire hunter who had shot him – hadn't minded leaving bodies around, but maybe other vampire hunters had different methods, he thought. Could Tamburo have belonged to a secret society? Were there hunters spread out all over the country?

Jason pulled into his own driveway and shut off the ignition. He folded his arms on the steering wheel. Were there always going to be people trying to kill off every vampire on the planet? Were he and Sienna always going to be in danger from someone?

He rested his head on his arms. Was this going to be his life? All through college and everything after that?

If you want to be with Sienna, maybe it is, Jason thought. Was it worth it? Was *she* worth it?

He lifted up his head, the answer instantaneous: hell, yeah, she was worth it. There was no way he was ever giving her up. 'So go ahead and bring it on,' he muttered. 'Whoever you are.'

Eight

Normal, Jason thought as he headed across the DeVere High courtyard the next day. *Here I am, acting normal.*

His body jerked as a hand slid up his back. Jason whipped round to see Sienna. 'At least I didn't squeal,' he said. 'You have to admit, I didn't make a sound of any kind.'

'We're all a little jumpy today,' Sienna reassured him.

Jason checked the clock tower. Still ten minutes before first period. He sat down on the closest stone bench. Sienna took a seat next to him. The palm fronds over their heads rattled gently in the slight breeze.

'I was thinking, would it be useful to bring the police in on this?' Jason asked her. 'Van Dyke's a missing minor. They'd get right on it. Maybe they could find out something. And it's not like absolutely everything that happens in Malibu has to do with *your* people.'

'Great minds,' Sienna said. 'I asked Zach pretty much the same thing about an hour ago. He told me that his sources go deeper and wider than the police's, and that getting the police involved could make it more complicated for us to do what we need to do – whatever that turns out to be. You know how Zach is. He doesn't exactly tell you everything on his mind.'

Jason nodded. 'I guess Zach's sources haven't . . . ?'

'Nothing yet,' Sienna replied. 'We were up all night, imagining all these terrible things that could have happened to him.'

'Sounds like quite a slumber party,' Jason commented.

'It's so weird being here today, isn't it?' Sienna asked, watching groups of kids go by, talking and laughing. 'Only a few of us know anything is wrong. To everybody else this is a totally normal day. Better than normal because school is almost out. If people notice Van Dyke isn't here, they'll just think he has a bad case of senioritis and is cutting class to go out and have fun.'

Whereas in reality he could be hurt, Jason silently added. *Maybe dead.*

Sometimes Malibu didn't seem like a place where people could die. It was naturally beautiful to begin with, but it had been shined and buffed and glossed until it was almost artificial. And maybe that was the point. When you were rich enough to live in Malibu, you could almost pretend the real world didn't exist.

You could almost pretend that shiny, glossy, beautiful – plus safe and happy – was reality.

But the same ugly things happened in Malibu that happened in the rest of the world: illness, crime, divorce, death, even murder. Once Jason had almost fallen over the dead body of a murdered girl right on a stretch of beach so pretty it should have been on a postcard. Living here was no protection.

'I guess we should head in,' Sienna said as the crowd around them thinned out.

'I guess,' Jason agreed. They stood up and walked out of the sun and into one of the cool, dim walkways that ran through the school. 'See you in English,' he said when they reached the stone stairway he had to take to get to his world history class. Sienna gave a little wave as he started up the stairs.

He reached the classroom with only seconds to spare before the second bell. Not that even the teachers could get themselves to care about that too much at this point. They were as ready for summer as every-body else.

Mr Munro took roll, then popped in a DVD after handing out a sheet of questions that would be answered during the DVD viewing. He looked as tired as Brad and Maggie did. Jason wondered how long they'd stayed out searching for Van Dyke last night. He knew they hadn't found even a hint about what had happened. Sienna would have called if they had.

Jason picked up his pen and read the first question. Mr Munro was cool about putting the questions in the order the info was given in the DVDs. Basically, all you had to do was stay awake to fill out the sheet – though that was sometimes not the easiest thing first period, especially with the lights dimmed.

A folded scrap of paper landed on his desk as he waited for the answer to question number one. He opened it after shooting a quick look at Mr Munro. The note was from Adam: 'What happened yesterday?'

Like Jason was going to start writing stuff down about the vampires and passing it over to Adam, who sat almost all the way across the room from him. He shook his head at his friend.

He heard the word 'Mesopotamian'. Damn, he'd missed the factoid he needed for the worksheet. He read the second question and got ready to listen for the answer.

Another note arrived from Adam: 'Did it have to do with Vs?' Jason crumpled it and focused on the photographs slowly flashing across the TV screen. He hoped Adam would interpret the message correctly as 'not now'.

Maybe he should have sent the message in Morse

code, because Adam didn't seem to pick up on the paper crumpling. Another note arrived less than a minute later that read: 'Let me help.'

Jason tore off a scrap of paper from the bottom of the worksheet. 'Later' he wrote on it. As he folded it, he heard the words 'cult of Anu'. Crap, he'd missed the second answer.

Screw it, he thought as he sent the note off across the room to Adam. *It's not like CalTech is going to find out that I didn't pay attention to the DVD and come tear up my acceptance letter.* At least, he hoped not.

'You two have P.E. this period, don't you?' Coach Middleton asked, catching up with Jason and Brad in the hall after world history.

'Yep,' Jason answered.

'Well, whatever they have you doing in there today, don't do it. I want you to get your swim team lockers cleaned out. I'm going to start working with the new guys over the summer and I need the space,' the coach told them. 'Don't get all sappy and nostalgic on me. You have fifty minutes. That's more than enough time. Tell Van Dyke to get his crap out of there too. Where is he anyway? He's supposed to have P.E. first period.'

'Uh, I saw him yesterday and he wasn't feeling that great. Maybe he decided to stay home,' Jason said.

'Seniors,' Coach Middleton snorted. 'Well, you call him on his cell and tell him to get his ass over here and get his locker cleaned out. I'm talking spotless or he'll be spending the summer swimming laps.' He veered off into one of the teachers' lounges.

'I guess we can pack Van Dyke's stuff up for him,' Jason suggested. He shot a look at Brad, wondering how he was doing.

'I know his locker combination,' Brad answered without emotion as they continued on.

Once they were inside the locker room, they found cardboard boxes waiting for them. Jason's locker was a row over from Brad's. They worked mostly in silence, separated by a wall of metal. Jason threw out a few comments, but Brad answered in monosyllables.

It didn't take Jason long to load up his gear. He didn't keep a ton of stuff at school. Goggles. Shampoo. Flip-flops. A couple of T-shirts and some shorts. A couple of swimsuits and a towel. Combined, it didn't even fill up half of one of the boxes.

Jason slammed his locker – he wanted to give Brad a head's up that he was finished – and circled around to see how Brad was doing. He had his gear boxed up too. He was sitting in front of Van Dyke's closed locker – the one right next to his – staring at it. Jason had the urge to back away, feeling like he'd walked in on something really private. But it was too late. Brad looked up and saw him standing there.

'Want some help?' Jason asked, trying to make the best of the situation.

Brad shrugged. But Jason's words got him moving. He dialed the combination into the lock and pulled it off, then opened the locker door. But he didn't start taking stuff out. Jason wondered if that would feel like giving up to Brad, like admitting that Van Dyke wouldn't be coming back to do it himself.

Jason was just about to make an excuse to give Brad some space, when Brad slammed the locker door shut. He pulled back his fist and rammed it into his own locker, leaving a crater. 'Whoever has Van Dyke better pray Zach finds them before I do,' Brad burst out, the muscles in his neck tense. He slammed the locker door again and strode away.

Zach was definitely more cool-headed. But Jason wasn't at all sure that that meant his punishment of whoever had Van Dyke would be any less severe.

He considered his options, then decided to clean out Van Dyke's locker himself. Zach didn't want Van Dyke's disappearance to become an issue, and it would become one with the coach if the locker wasn't dealt with.

Jason opened Van Dyke's locker door and moved a

cardboard box in front of it. *When Van Dyke gets back, I'm going to have to give him some serious grief about the number of hair and skin products he has in here*, Jason thought, hoping he would get that opportunity.

Jason loaded half a dozen fancy little bottles into Van Dyke's box, each one designed to keep hair or skin free from the ravages of chlorine.

'Need any help?' came Adam's voice suddenly.

Jason glanced over his shoulder, surprised to see his best friend. 'What are you doing in here? You don't have P.E. now. And I know you never choose to hang out in the locker room of your own free will.'

Adam held up a bathroom pass. 'It's later. And I wanted to make sure that we aren't in the middle of an emergency I need to know about.'

'The short version is that Van Dyke went missing from his own barbecue,' Jason explained. 'He went to pick up Maggie, and never got there. Nobody's heard from him since.'

'You guys don't want to get my dad involved? You do have a close personal connection to the Chief of Police,' Adam reminded him.

'We're not sure exactly what, uh, elements are involved here,' Jason said. 'Zach wants to keep it quiet until he can find out more.'

'OK.' Adam dug around in his pocket, then pulled

out a pill and stuck it in his mouth. 'My dad's on this vitamin kick,' he explained, in response to Jason's puzzled look. 'He's somehow rationalized eating a diet that's ninety per cent junk food as long as he takes this massive assortment of vitamins, and now he has me taking them too. The up side – I get to have potato chips for breakfast.'

'I wouldn't mind that plan.'

'So, anyway, there's nothing I can do?' Adam asked.

'Well, you can carry one of these boxes over to the door. I'll throw them in my car after school,' Jason said, more because he wanted to give Adam some way to help out than because he actually needed help. 'Other than that, our big assignment from Zach is to act normal.'

'Act normal,' Adam repeated, grabbing the closest box. 'I'll do my best.'

'Well, we made it through the day,' Sienna said as she and Brad caught up to Jason in the hall after last class. 'We came to school like it was any other day.'

'It felt about ten times as long, though,' Brad commented.

'Yeah,' Jason agreed.

'I talked to Zach in chem,' Sienna told them. 'He wants us to meet up at my place for a strategy session.

Belle and I are going to do a quick food run on the way there. Two nights of slumber partying emptied the kitchen.'

'Good. I want to meet,' Brad said.

'I'm going to grab the junk from my locker and dump it at home, then I'll be over,' Jason told her. He gave her a quick kiss goodbye.

'Yeah, I'll come with you. I'll get my stuff and Van Dyke's,' Brad said. They walked down the corridor in silence. The school was already mostly empty. This late in the year there were no activities to keep anybody around.

Brad stopped short about six feet from the double doors leading into the gym. 'Do you see that?'

Jason followed his gaze. Brad was staring at the ground.

'I don't see anything,' Jason said.

Brad took a couple of steps forward and crouched down. 'Right there. It's blood.'

Jason knelt next to him. Now he could see a small smear of dark red.

'It's fresh,' Brad told him.

'So someone stubbed their toe,' Jason suggested, straightening up.

'There's too much. There's a lot of it. I can smell it. You can't smell it?' Brad darted forward. 'There's some more.' He pointed to another smear along the bottom of the wall a few feet closer to the gym.

Brad rushed along the trail of almost imperceptible – at least to Jason – drops and stains of blood. It led around the gym to the locker room. Brad held one arm out, cautioning Jason, and pointed to a thin streak of blood on the long metal door handle. 'Watch yourself. We don't know what's going to be in here.'

Slowly Brad opened the door. Jason strained to catch any sounds from inside. He could hear the shower running.

Brad moved toward the sound, fast and silent as a panther. Jason followed as quietly as he could. When Brad rounded the entrance to the showers, he stopped dead and let out a sound like he'd been punched in the gut. Jason looked around him and sucked in his breath with a hiss.

Van Dyke was huddled on the tiled floor, shirtless but still wearing his pants, the shower water streaming down onto him. Blood and dirt mingled in the water and swirled away down the plug. The water was obviously warm because steam filled the room, and yet Van Dyke was shivering violently. Brad raced to his side, turning off the water, while Jason ran to grab a towel from the stuff he'd cleared out of his locker.

Jason returned and helped Brad to wrap the towel

around Van Dyke's shoulders. Jason could see that his feet were bare and bleeding, one of his fingernails was halfway ripped off and his pants were torn. Despite the shower, some grime still streaked his chest and there was a perfectly round wound on his abdomen. A section of his scalp had been shaved and there was a neat row of stitches across it.

'Who did this to you?' Brad cried. 'Van Dyke, who in the hell did this to you?'

Who could *have done this?* Jason wondered. *Who could have been strong enough to do* all this *to a vampire?*

Nine

'Who did this to you?' Brad shouted again.

Van Dyke didn't answer. He just groaned weakly and pulled the towel more tightly around himself.

Brad sucked in a deep breath. When he spoke again, his voice was gentle. 'I'm going to take care of you, buddy,' Brad told Van Dyke. Calmly, he pulled out his cell and punched in a number.

'Who are you calling?' Jason demanded.

'School nurse,' Brad answered.

'Isn't this a little out of her league? We need an ambulance. EMTs,' Jason protested.

'Can you come to the boys' locker room? There's been an accident. Nothing too serious. Some minor cuts. Thanks,' Brad said into the phone.

Has he gone into shock? Jason wondered, staring at Brad.

Brad took him by the arm. 'This is what he *needs*.'

Finally, it clicked in Jason's head. He got it. Van Dyke was dangerously weak. What he needed was blood.

Brad had called the nurse so Van Dyke could feed on her. 'Sorry.' Jason shook his head. 'I wasn't thinking.'

'Why don't you go wait over by the lockers? I'll wait with Michael,' Brad said. Jason realized it was the first time he'd ever heard Brad call Van Dyke by his first name.

'Sure.' Jason automatically headed over to his own locker and sat down on the wooden bench in front of it. He knew all about the realities of vampire blood-drinking. But there was a part of him that was still deeply uncomfortable with the fact, even though he knew, knew from actual experience, that it was extremely pleasurable when a vampire fed on a human, and that the vampires never took enough blood to do any harm. Only a rogue vampire *drained* the donor when he drank.

About five minutes later, Jason heard the nurse hurry into the locker room. Heard Brad direct her to the showers. Then, about five minutes after that, he saw Brad and Van Dyke walk her back out into the main part of the locker room, and saw the dazed and happy expression on her face as they easily convinced her that Van Dyke was absolutely fine and his parents didn't need to be contacted.

As soon as she was gone, Van Dyke's pleasant expression hardened. 'We need to get everyone together,' he declared. '*Now!*'

* * *

Jason called Sienna as he strode across the parking lot to the VW. 'Change of plans. We're meeting at Van Dyke's place in an hour. He's back. He's going to tell us everything when we all get there.'

Sienna hung up almost immediately so she could pass on the news. Jason hit Adam's speed dial number.

'What's going on?' Adam asked as soon as he picked up.

'Just wanted to tell you I can't do *Reservoir Dogs* tonight,' Jason said.

'Oh. That's . . . OK. I figured it was off, with everything else that's going down,' Adam answered.

'Yeah, I figured you'd figured, but I wanted to make sure. Also, Van Dyke is back.'

'He is? Where was he? What happened to him?' Adam asked in a rush.

'I don't really know yet. I'm not even sure how much he knows. He was hurt pretty bad,' Jason said. 'We're meeting up at his place in an hour and he's going to fill us in as much as he can.'

'I'll be there.' Adam hung up before Jason could say that maybe that wasn't a good idea.

Except it actually *was* a good idea. Adam had come through for the vampires in lots of ways this past year. Zach had even pretty much said so at Brad's party.

They'd probably be glad to have him around tonight. In Jason's opinion, they were in a we-need-all-the-help-we-can-get situation.

'Start from the beginning. We need to understand as much about the situation as we can,' Zach told Van Dyke when everyone in the group was gathered. Everybody seemed fine with Adam being there. It had only been awkward on the weekend because he'd had Brianna with him.

Van Dyke wiped his face with his fingers. 'I'll try. But I'm telling you right now I don't remember everything.' He sucked in a deep breath. 'So, the beginning: I get a call from Maggie.' He reached out and took her hand. 'I start driving over there. On the way, there's an accident blocking the road. I can see a body on the street.'

Jason heard Belle give a little gasp.

'I pulled over and ran to check on the guy. I wasn't sure if he was still alive. I had my cell out. I was about to call 911. But when I leant down to check his pulse, he sat up and zapped me with some kind of stun gun,' Van Dyke explained.

Brad looked like he badly wanted to punch something again. Jason felt the same way.

'When you get hit with one of those, your whole

nervous system gets disabled. Human or vampire,' Van Dyke continued. 'So I'm on the ground. I can't move. And five guys – I think five – pour out of the van. I forgot to say that one of the vehicles in the accident was a van,' Van Dyke added, turning to Zach. 'The guys had me in the back in seconds and we were out of there.'

'One of them must have driven your car off,' Brad said. 'There was no sign of it when we followed your route to Maggie's house.'

'They really had the whole thing planned out,' Jason added. 'Not just staging the accident, but slashing Maggie's tires. They must know you're her boyfriend and figured that she'd call you for a ride. They knew exactly which streets you'd take to get to her place, too.' *They aren't going to be easy to stop*, he thought.

'They have to have been watching us closely to know all that. I don't like it,' Belle said.

'That's the kind of information we need about them. That kind of detail,' Zach told them, his voice cold.

Zach's not going to be easy to stop, either, Jason acknowledged. He looked around the room. At Brad's clenched fists. Maggie's tight jaw. Erin's ramrod straight posture. Sienna's blazing eyes. None of them would be easy to stop. They were all pissed off. Even Zach in his own icy way. And Belle, scared as she was.

One of their own had been hurt and someone was going to pay.

'What do you remember about where you were held?' Zach asked Van Dyke.

'My cell was small,' he answered slowly.

'Cell!' Belle exclaimed, outraged.

'It was . . . maybe . . . nine by six,' Van Dyke continued. 'A cot. A bucket. Damp. Smelly, obviously. It's weird, because other parts of the place were really hi-tech. They brought me into operating rooms a couple of times.'

Jason saw Sienna's face pale. His hand drifted to the spot on his head that had been shaved on Van Dyke's. When he realized what he'd done, he jammed his hand in his pocket.

'Were the people who captured you human?' Brad asked.

'Yeah. But they had some hi-tech equipment. They strapped me on a gurney to move me and the straps were made of nothing I've ever seen before. Like something from a space shuttle. I couldn't make even a tiny tear in them. Sometimes they half knocked me out with gas. Every time they wanted me not to use my strength, they gassed me.' Van Dyke stared blankly into space for a moment. It seemed like he was focusing on a memory. Then he gave his head a brisk shake. 'Like I said, I wasn't always conscious, but I know they drew a lot of blood from me, and they took some spinal fluid. And they kept sticking me with these long needles. Not injecting me. Pulling stuff out.'

'It sounds like they were doing biopsies of your organs,' Adam said. 'They were doing a real workup on you.'

'Is that what happened to his head? A brain biopsy?' Erin asked.

'Maybe,' Adam replied.

'How did you get out of there?' Maggie asked Van Dyke. Her eyes shimmered with tears she wasn't allowing herself to shed.

'They have another vampire,' Van Dyke told the group. 'I should have said that right up front. Christopher. I've never seen him around here before.' Again his gaze went to Zach. 'I think they've had him for a while. He doesn't look too good. But he managed to pass me a key to the handcuffs they used.'

'How did he get that?' Zach asked.

'I'm not sure,' Van Dyke answered. 'I'm not sure about anything. We didn't have the chance to talk much. Anyway, they were going to do some experiments on me – something where they had to take me outside the main location. They put the cuffs on and put me back in the van. They weren't paying as much attention to me, because they were sure I was restrained and the van was moving. So I used the key to get the cuffs off, yanked open the door and jumped.'

'Obviously, we don't have any time to waste,' Zach announced. 'One of us is still being held captive. We don't know how long he can survive, so we have to rescue him. We have to find the place where Van Dyke was held and shut it down before it's too late.'

'So you think you were held in a warehouse . . .' Zach recapped, as Brad slipped out of the room.

'The place was big, that's for sure,' Van Dyke answered. 'And my cell felt like a warehouse, cold and damp. Definitely not heated like a building that was used by a lot of people. At least, not that part of it.'

'Did you see anything that made you think you were being held by vampire hunters like Tamburo?' Jason asked. 'Any ritualistic objects? Anything with the phases of the moon as symbols?'

Van Dyke shook his head. 'All the equipment these guys had was really hi-tech,' he said, pacing back and forth across the living room. His wounds had visibly improved and he was clearly eager to go out and kick some ass. 'The stuff could have come out of your dad's labs, Sienna. It was that cutting edge. Some of the tech guys were even wearing what looked like hazmat suits. This wasn't some rinky-dink operation.'

Brad hurried back into the living room. 'I snagged this from the study,' he said, spreading a detailed map of Malibu out on the coffee table. 'I thought it could help. Let's go over everything you remember about your escape. You said you jumped out of the van. Can you show us where on the map?'

Van Dyke sat on the floor and leant over the coffee table. 'I hit the ground hard and rolled. I was going to try to stand up and start running, but I picked up momentum. It turned out there was a hill at the side of the road. A steep, scrubby hill. And I was going down it whether I wanted to or not. When I finally stopped, I got up and ran.'

'I'm thinking the school must have been closer than your house and that's why you went there,' Brad suggested.

'Yeah,' Van Dyke agreed.

'Any idea how far you ran?' Jason asked.

'It felt like a marathon. But maybe a mile. At least a mile,' Van Dyke answered.

Van Dyke studied the map. 'Here's the school.' He tapped the map. 'And I think this has got to be the hill.' He tapped it again. 'So this has to be where I jumped out of the van.' He pointed to a road.

'Now we just need to work back from there,' Sienna

said. 'How long do you think you rode in the van before the heroic leap?'

'I probably had a brain biopsy before this all happened,' Van Dyke reminded everyone.

'Best guess,' Erin urged.

'Twenty minutes,' Van Dyke told them.

'And how fast do you think the van was going?' Jason asked.

'This is starting to feel like one of those word problems from the third grade. I never liked those,' Van Dyke complained. 'When I jumped out, it felt as though we were going about forty. Let's say we were going around forty the whole time. I don't remember speeding up or slowing down a whole lot.'

'Twenty minutes, forty miles an hour,' Brad muttered. Then he drew a large circle around the place Van Dyke estimated he'd rolled down the hill. 'This is the area we're looking at,' he told the group. 'We're trying to come up with a large building, like a warehouse, somewhere near the perimeter of the circle.'

'More or less,' Van Dyke added.

'Right,' Brad agreed.

'I can't think of a large building anywhere out there. But I don't know that many large buildings that don't sell stuff,' Belle admitted apologetically.

'Maybe we can narrow it down some more,' Jason

said. 'Think about smells and sounds and anything you caught sight of from the van windows. Say whatever comes into your head. It might make one of us think of something.'

Van Dyke frowned, tapping his fingers on the map. 'This isn't a sight or sound or smell, but the road was mostly smooth,' he said.

'That eliminates the northernmost part of the circle.' Zach shaded that section with a pencil. 'The roads up there are bumpy as hell.'

'Excellent!' Maggie cried. 'What else?' she asked Van Dyke.

'I couldn't see much from the back of the van. They had me flat on my back. But I know the driver had to stop twice to open gates so that we could keep going,' Van Dyke said.

'Gates.' Sienna tapped her bottom lip. 'Did you hear any water around that time?'

'Yeah!' Van Dyke exclaimed. 'Why do you ask that?'

'Because Vera Canyon has smooth roads. They repaved them about two months ago. And there are some gated sections, and waterfalls leading into Zuma Creek,' Sienna explained.

'That could be right. I couldn't see much from the van, but I did see a lot of tree branches,' Van Dyke told her.

'Down in Vera Canyon there are places where the trees practically make a tunnel!' Erin added, her voice filled with excitement.

'OK, so we know we need to go this way to get to the warehouse or whatever building Van Dyke was held in.' Brad traced a line from the hill over to Vera Canyon. 'We still have eight or so miles to figure out.'

'I'm trying to think of other stuff,' Van Dyke said, his eyes closed. The room fell silent as everyone willed him to remember something. 'You know, there was this weird smell,' he said after a moment. 'I first noticed it not long after we'd started out. Maybe only four or five miles from the warehouse.'

'What was it like?' Maggie asked.

'It's hard to describe. I've definitely smelled it before, but it's not common,' Van Dyke answered. He took a long sniff, like he was trying to suck in the odor again. 'The circus,' he said. 'It smelled like the circus.'

'What part of the circus?' Erin asked. 'Like the popcorn and peanuts?'

'Or sawdust?' Brad suggested.

'I bet I know!' Belle exclaimed. 'I bet you were smelling the Hollywood Star ranch. That's the place where they keep all the exotic animals that are trained for the movies.' Belle turned to Maggie. 'Remember, our girl scout troop went there in the fourth grade?'

'Oh, right. That place definitely smelled. They had some big animals too. Elephants and everything – like at a circus.' Maggie pulled the map a little closer to her. 'The ranch is right about here.' She pointed to a spot that was very near part of the circle's perimeter.

'It was kind of a funky animal smell,' Van Dyke confirmed. 'That could be it.'

'I've been to the ranch, too,' Brad said. 'I'm pretty sure there's an abandoned warehouse close by. I vaguely remember seeing one.'

'Yeah. There's some kind of big building up there. I shot some footage of it once,' Adam added. 'I remember thinking it might be a good location for something. It's built into the hillside.' He pointed at the map. 'About *there.*'

Jason could feel expectation rising up in him. He looked around the group. They were feeling it too

'To me it sounds like a good location to kick some ass,' Van Dyke declared.

Ten

'Let's go,' Zach said.

Jason glanced at him in surprise. 'Go? Where?'

'To that warehouse.' Zach's voice was hard. 'And if it's the same place where Van Dyke was held, we're going to shut it down.' Zach got to his feet, joining Brad and Van Dyke, who were already up and ready to go.

'Hold on,' Jason protested. 'Don't you think we need to plan this out a little better?'

'No,' Zach replied. 'The assholes who took Van Dyke know that he's escaped. They're probably out there looking for him, right now. Looking for all of us, maybe.'

'Yeah. The sooner we get rid of them, the better,' Brad muttered. 'Then we can all stop living in fear.'

'I agree,' Jason said. 'But—'

'With the rest of the council unreachable, it's up to us to handle this,' Zach reminded him. 'So let's go handle it.'

Van Dyke cracked his neck. 'My pleasure,' he said grimly.

Jason sensed a strange undercurrent of excitement in Van Dyke's voice, and he glanced over at him. *Van Dyke looks good*, Jason thought, startled. *Vampire good.* The guy was practically glowing, his hair shiny, his cheekbones sharp enough to cut someone. Jason turned to Zach and Brad. Same thing. They'd let their regular 'human' appearance slide a bit, and he could swear they actually looked bigger than usual.

'Uh, guys?' he said. 'You want to tell me why you're going all superhuman?'

Zach stared at Jason for a moment, his brown eyes glinting, looking almost black. Then his face seemed to soften, his wiry frame taking on a more normal look. His eyes lightened, slightly. He was regular Zach again – or as regular as the guy ever got.

'We're just pumped up is all,' Brad muttered, returning his appearance to normal. Van Dyke didn't change a bit.

'I get that,' Jason said. 'Believe me, I want to find the guys that took Van Dyke as much as you do. But when you get all vampired-up, it makes me think you might forget yourselves.'

'We're wasting time,' Van Dyke growled.

'Look, I know how strong you are,' Jason told him.

'And it's OK to beat up those jerks. But it's not OK to kill them.'

'We can control ourselves,' Zach said shortly. 'Van Dyke.'

'Fine.' Slowly, Van Dyke returned his appearance to normal. 'Now, let's go.'

'You're all acting crazy,' Sienna said. 'We have no idea if there's even a warehouse there, it's dark out, and we haven't even driven by to see if Van Dyke is sure it's the right place. We should come up with a strategy.'

'The strategy is simple. We get over there, I see if it's the place, and if it is we tear it down and take care of the guys running it,' Van Dyke said angrily.

'What do you mean, take care of them?' Belle asked.

'What do you think he means?' Brad demanded. 'These people *experimented* on him.'

'And they're probably still torturing Christopher,' Van Dyke put in. 'That dude saved my life! I'm not waiting. I'm taking them out the first chance I get.'

'The three of us are more than a match for half a dozen humans,' Zach said brusquely. 'If they know what's good for them, they won't try to stop us.'

'Yeah, we can just burn the lab down and ruin all their research,' Brad said.

Sienna still looked concerned. 'So, no hurting anybody?'

'And what's with the "three"?' demanded Maggie angrily. 'We're also vampire-strong – we're coming along too!'

'Better not,' Zach pointed out drily. 'These are *humans*, remember? We can't take the risk of exposure that girls along would lead to – you know that, Maggie.'

'Anyway, they're not gonna learn their lesson unless we rough them up a little,' Van Dyke continued. 'Believe me, they deserve it.'

'Come on.' Zach headed for the door without another glance at Sienna's worried face.

Whoever experimented on Van Dyke deserves at least a punch or two, Jason thought. But if the vampires did more than that, word could get out and then there would be trouble.

But when Brad and Van Dyke started after Zach, Jason went along with them. If his friends got too hot-headed, maybe he'd be able to stop them somehow.

Zach glanced over and caught his eye. For a brief moment, Jason got the distinct feeling that he wasn't welcome in this little posse. But he held Zach's gaze and, eventually, Zach nodded.

As Jason reached the door, Sienna grabbed his hand.

'Be careful,' she said, her voice tense. 'I don't like this. I wish I could come with you.'

'Don't worry,' he said. 'I'll be extra-careful. And I'll try to make sure everyone else is, too.'

Over her shoulder, he caught a glimpse of Adam staring at him open-mouthed. His best friend clearly thought that Jason had lost his mind, tagging along with a bunch of vampires on an illegal search-and-destroy mission.

Jason pulled the door closed behind him, hoping that Adam was wrong.

These vampires are freaking me out, Jason thought wryly as Brad drove through the dark Malibu night. He'd been hanging around the toothy types for so long now that he usually didn't even think of them as being different from him. But tonight there was a strange energy in the car, and it definitely wasn't normal.

Nobody had said a word since they left Van Dyke's house. But the air throbbed with intensity. The three vampires were so filled with anger that Jason could feel it in his own body. The road they were on climbed up the side of a hill, twisting and turning back on itself over and over as it ascended. There were no houses, and the inky blackness seemed to press in around the headlights.

'We're almost at the top,' Zach said, his voice loud in the silence. 'Park out of sight.'

Brad nodded and pulled to the side of the narrow road. A small stand of trees blocked their view over the edge of the hill, and also blocked the car from the sight of anyone lower down on the hillside. As the guys climbed out of the car, Jason realized that his heart was beating fast. Were they in the right place? Would they really be able to find Van Dyke's captors and rescue the other vampire?

'The building we're aiming for is sort of built into the hillside, like Adam said,' Brad reminded them. 'We can check it out from behind the trees, see if there's anyone there.'

They crept over to the trees and peered down into the darkness. Jason could just make out the dark outline of a large, low building. Only one light was on, a pale yellow security bulb over the doorway.

'It does look like a warehouse,' Jason murmured. 'But it also looks pretty empty. I think it's abandoned.'

'What do you think, Van Dyke?' Zach asked. 'Does anything look familiar?'

Van Dyke squinted into the darkness, then slowly shook his head. 'I don't know. I honestly can't remember a thing about the outside of the place.'

We should creep down the hill, get a closer look, Jason thought. *Maybe something would spark Van Dyke's memory.* But before he could even suggest it, Brad was heading for the open hillside.

'There's one way to find out if it's the right place,' he called over his shoulder.

'Yeah. Let's go.' Van Dyke took off after him, and Zach followed. Jason watched them, surprised. 'I guess we're not being stealthy,' he muttered as he went after his friends.

The hillside wasn't as steep as it looked from above, and it only took them a minute or two to reach the driveway leading to the old warehouse. A van was parked out front, but otherwise the drive was empty.

'It's quiet,' Brad commented.

'That doesn't mean there's nobody home,' Jason said.

Zach took a step forward.

Suddenly a white light snapped on with a metallic clanging sound. Jason winced as the brightness stabbed into his eyeballs. A second later, another light clanged on. The dark hillside was as bright as daylight – and Jason felt as if two fake suns were aimed right at him. Spots swam in front of his eyes.

'What the hell?' Brad complained, shading his own eyes.

'I see six of them,' Zach said quietly, staring into the lights.

Jason squinted at the building. Zach was right – there were six dark shapes silhouetted against the brightness. Six *large* dark shapes.

'This is private property!' a gruff voice called. 'Get out!'

'For an abandoned warehouse, it's got some pretty tough security,' Jason said.

'Who's in charge here?' Zach called, stepping forward. Jason had to hand it to the guy – he wasn't squinting, or covering his eyes, and he seemed completely cool and in control. Well, why not? Jason thought. *Six humans are still no match for three vampires.*

'I said *leave*. You're trespassing,' the gruff voice replied, in a thick New York accent.

'I'll leave after I talk to the man in charge,' Zach said. 'Who's running this operation?'

There were a few chuckles from the darkened figures. 'There's no operation,' the New Yorker replied. 'This is a toy warehouse. You want to buy some *Dora the Explorer* dolls?'

'They're lying,' Van Dyke whispered. 'I recognize that guy's voice, his accent. He's definitely one of the dudes who was holding me captive.'

'Good,' Zach said. 'I was getting sick of this small talk, anyway.' Zach was already striding forward, Van

Dyke and Brad half a step behind him.

'Forward!' the New Yorker growled, and the six security guys rushed to meet them. Even as he got ready for a fight, Jason felt shocked. If these were the people who'd taken Van Dyke captive, that meant they knew about vampires. And they obviously knew about the vampires' strength, otherwise they wouldn't have kept Van Dyke sedated. So why were they rushing in to fight not one, but *three* vampires? And for all they knew, Jason was a vampire, too.

They're crazy, Jason thought. *They think they can win by outnumbering the vampires. They don't know what they're in for.*

In the glare of the spotlights, the humans and vampires came together, and for a few seconds Jason lost track of his friends. A bunch of darkened figures grappled together. He moved closer, looking for one of the security goons to take down. His friends could handle two humans each with no problem, but Jason was determined to help them anyway.

There was a loud grunt, and the sound of fist slamming into flesh. Somebody yelled in pain, and a big guy came flying toward Jason.

He leapt out of the way just as the huge dude hit the ground, blood spraying from his mouth.

One down, Jason thought, stepping over the security

guard. He glanced down to make sure the guy wasn't going to be getting up again any time soon – and stopped, astonished.

The guy on the ground was Van Dyke.

Eleven

Jason locked eyes with Van Dyke. 'What the hell?' he gasped.

Van Dyke frowned. 'Dunno,' he grunted, pushing himself back to his feet. 'They're strong.' Shaking it off, he rushed back into the blinding lights, where Brad and Zach were still fighting with the six human guys.

Jason ran after him. Closer up, he had a better view of the humans. They were all big dudes, but none of them had weapons. They were just fighting hand to hand with the vampires.

And they were winning.

Did we get it wrong? Jason wondered. *Are these security guys vampires, too?*

But even though they were strong, none of the security men *looked* like vampires. Not one of them had the sort of glow that Zach, Brad and Van Dyke had shown earlier.

'Van Dyke,' Jason called, running into the fray. 'Are these guys . . . like you?'

Van Dyke didn't even look at him, he was too busy trading punches with a dark-haired security dude. 'No. No way,' he grunted.

Jason tried to figure out how he could best help. His friends were being pummeled.

Brad took a forearm to the jaw that snapped his head around. Before he could recover, the guy fighting him threw a punch into Brad's gut. The vampire doubled over, gasping for breath.

On the other side of Jason, Zach was trading blows with the New Yorker, who was the biggest of the humans. Zach got in a few good punches, but the big guy didn't even seem to feel them. As Jason watched, he casually backhanded Zach across the face, then followed up with a sucker punch to the side of Zach's head.

Dazed, Zach stumbled into Jason. Jason grabbed his arm to steady him, but Zach looked pretty out of it. The New Yorker was heading right for them.

Jason stepped in front of Zach and threw up his arm just in time. The New Yorker's huge fist slammed into Jason's arm with an incredible amount of force, but Jason managed to hold strong. He ducked and ran head-first at the guy's stomach, tackling him to the ground.

Jason landed on top of him and immediately

reached back to hit the guy in the face. But the New Yorker grabbed his arm before the blow even fell. He bent Jason's wrist back until Jason cried out in pain, rolling off him.

The man immediately jumped back to his feet and rushed at Zach again.

Jason took off after him. His wrist still ached, but Zach couldn't take this guy alone. Running up behind the man, Jason snaked his arm around the guy's neck, secured his hold with his other hand, and squeezed. As the New Yorker tried to pry Jason off his back, Zach pummeled his torso with punches that would've floored a normal human.

The New Yorker bellowed in rage and spun away, moving faster than Jason thought possible for such a big guy. The sheer velocity of the movement made him lose his hold on the dude's neck. The guy grabbed Jason's arm and yanked, pulling Jason off of him and sending him flying through the air.

Slam! Jason's back hit something hard and cold, and he fell to the ground, winded.

I've got to get up before he comes after me again, Jason thought. But he couldn't move. He could barely breathe. He dragged himself to a sitting position and looked up. A black van loomed above him, the metal side dented where he had slammed into it. Jason shook his head, trying to think clearly. Maybe he could use the van as cover if the New Yorker came for him.

Jason glanced back to the fight. The New Yorker was still battling it out with Zach, both of them moving so quickly that they were a blur.

He doesn't care about me, Jason realized. *He's only interested in taking down Zach.* In fact, all six humans were busy fighting Zach, Brad and Van Dyke. None of them paid any attention to Jason at all.

They must know I'm human, he thought. He wasn't a threat to them, so they weren't bothering to go after him.

But the vampires didn't seem like much of a threat to these guys, either. Whenever the New Yorker stopped hitting Zach, one of the other dudes started in. Van Dyke was on his knees, two big guys raining punches on his head.

They have to be vampires, Jason thought. How else could the dudes be pounding on his friends this way? Maybe Van Dyke had got it wrong.

Brad let out a cry of pain, snapping Jason back to attention. Human or vampire, these guys were destroying Jason's friends. He had to help them.

Jason got to his feet and waded back into the battle. One of the guys beating on Brad had his back to Jason. Jason leapt up and shot a fast kick into his kidneys. It wasn't a fair kick, but these security guys had been fighting dirty right from the start. Jason figured he and his friends were going to have to do whatever it took to get out of here alive.

The guy hit the ground, moaning in pain. Brad shot Jason a grateful look, but he was too busy fending off the other guy to do more than that. Jason took a step toward them, but another security dude suddenly blocked his path.

'Get out of our way,' the guy muttered. He placed his hands on Jason's shoulder and shoved – hard.

For the second time in about three minutes, Jason was eating dirt. His whole ribcage felt bruised from the shock of being thrown around. At least this time he'd just landed on the ground instead of slamming into a car. Jason lay there for a moment, mentally checking himself for injuries. Once his head was clear, he dragged himself to his feet and looked around. These security dudes were too much, even for the vampires.

But would they even be able to make it to their car? Things looked bad. As Jason watched, Zach went down, the New Yorker on top of him. Van Dyke's face was covered in blood, and Brad was getting punched in the stomach, over and over, while only managing to get one or two return blows in.

This is no ordinary brawl, Jason thought. *My friends are really in danger.*

And then an engine roared to life. Jason's head snapped toward the sound, and he saw the black van's headlights come on. 'What now?' he muttered.

The engine revved loudly, then the van sped into the knot of fighters. Everybody scattered.

With a cry of surprise, the New Yorker jumped out of the way. The van squealed to a stop just inches from where Zach lay.

Jason blinked into the light. Was that . . . ?

'Get in!' Sienna yelled from behind the wheel. Belle sat beside her, gesturing frantically.

'Thank God,' Jason said. In a second, he was up and running toward Zach. 'Let's go! Let's go!' he called to the vampires.

Brad turned and stumbled toward the van as Jason grabbed Zach under the arms and dragged him to his feet. The security guys were already after them again. 'Van Dyke, come on!' Jason yelled.

The double doors at the back of the van opened with a *clang!* and Adam appeared, holding out a hand to Brad. The security dudes fell back as Brad got into the van, followed by Zach. Jason had to grab Van Dyke to keep him from going after the guys again, in spite of his bloody face.

'Get in the van,' Jason ordered him.

Reluctantly, Van Dyke climbed in. Jason followed, and he and Adam jerked the doors closed as Sienna tore away.

Nobody said a word as the van made its way up the winding drive to the top of the hill. Sienna pulled to the side of the road behind Brad's car, and cut the engine. The sound of crickets filled the air, and for a moment they all sat in the darkness, listening.

'Are they coming after us?' Jason asked.

'I don't hear anything,' Zach replied.

'Well, good then. Because you have super-hearing and all,' Adam joked nervously. 'So we must be safe.'

Jason threw open the back doors of the van, and they all climbed out. Sienna came around from the driver's side and slipped her arms around him. 'You OK?' she asked quietly.

'Yeah. They weren't interested in me,' Jason told her. He turned to the vampire guys. 'You three took a pretty bad beating. Everyone all right?'

Van Dyke wiped his face with his shirt. Jason was surprised to see that, once the blood was gone, he looked absolutely fine. 'We heal fast, remember? We'll be fine.'

'It might take me an hour or so,' Zach said wryly. 'That New York dude had it in for me. I'm glad you all showed up when you did.'

'What are you doing here, anyway?' Brad asked the girls.

'Sienna and I were worried about you,' Belle explained. 'Actually, we were worried about the humans. We thought you might get carried away and hurt somebody real bad. So Adam suggested that we come along ourselves and keep an eye on things.'

Jason glanced over Sienna's dark hair to see her Spider parked about twenty feet away.

'We got down to the warehouse just as you all started fighting,' Sienna said. 'We wanted to be around in case the humans needed help. But then it turned out that you were the ones who needed help. So Belle and I decided to commandeer the van to get us all out of there – fast.'

'I tried to get the girls to climb back up the hill so they'd be safe,' Adam told Jason. 'They ignored me.'

'Good thing they did,' Jason replied.

'I'll say,' Belle agreed. 'What on earth happened?'

'I'm not sure.' Zach rubbed his neck and winced. 'Those security guys weren't normal.'

'Are you absolutely positive they were human?' Jason asked. 'Because the only time I've ever been thrown around like that was when Luke Archer was doing the throwing.' The memory of fighting a bloodlusting vampire wasn't a pleasant one. But Jason couldn't help thinking about it tonight.

'Yeah, they definitely had vampire strength . . .' Brad said slowly.

'They're human,' Van Dyke declared firmly. 'They're the same guys who held me captive. Human.'

'I agree,' Zach said. 'I just didn't get any kind of a vampire sense from them. But they had the strength, and it's superhuman strength.'

'How can that be?' Sienna asked, her voice tense.

'That's what we have to find out,' Zach said. His eyes met Van Dyke's. 'Before we make our next attempt to rescue Christopher.'

Van Dyke looked as if he wanted to argue, but Brad nodded. 'Definitely. Next time we'll be prepared.' He turned to Van Dyke. 'Dude, I'm gonna stay at your place tonight, just in case they decide to show up. We'll all meet up tomorrow and devise our rescue plan.'

Slowly, Van Dyke nodded. Jason could see that he was still itching to get back there and save the vampire he'd left behind.

'Now let's get out of here,' Belle suggested. 'It creeps me out with them just down the hill.'

'What about the van?' Sienna asked. 'Should we just leave it here?'

'No, let's take it with us,' Jason replied. 'It was parked

at the warehouse. Maybe it will give us some
information about the operation they've got going
down there.'

'We can put it in my garage,' Van Dyke said.

'Good idea. I'll drive it back,' Zach said, heading for
the driver's side. Belle climbed in beside him as Brad
and Van Dyke headed for Brad's car.

Sienna slipped her arm around Jason's waist.

'Coming, Adam?' Brad called over his shoulder.

'I came with Sienna,' Adam said obliviously.

Van Dyke turned around, clapped his beefy arm
over Adam's shoulders, and steered him away from
Jason and Sienna.

'Oh. OK. Um . . . I'll catch a ride with these guys,'
Adam said.

'Great.' Jason grinned and waved as his best friend
was dragged off.

'You sure you're OK?' Sienna asked as they walked
toward her car.

'Well, I'll feel better once I see your car actually
start,' Jason teased her. 'What were you thinking,
driving all the way up here in that piece of junk?'

'I was thinking my boyfriend was here and he could
fix it,' she teased back. Then her expression grew
serious. 'Stay at my house tonight, Jason. Can you? I'd
feel better.'

'I thought all the girls were sleeping over,' Jason said.

'Even so, I'd rather have you there. It's been a really weird day.' Sienna leant against the car and turned toward him, pulling him against her. 'Of course, if you don't want to . . .'

'Oh, I want to.' Jason bent to brush his lips against hers, astonished to find himself so hot and bothered in spite of having been thrown against a van twenty minutes ago. 'But I'm kind of banged up. If I come home with you, will you kiss all my bruises and make them better?'

'I'll kiss whatever you want,' Sienna purred. She slipped out of his arms and got behind the wheel.

Jason climbed in next to her, his heart racing – and not from the recent fight. He could hardly wait to be alone with Sienna. The drive back to DeVere Heights seemed to take forever.

The other girls had set up camp in the living room and were busy watching *Smallville* DVDs.

'Don't mind us,' Maggie called teasingly as Sienna pulled Jason past them toward her room.

Inside, Jason pulled her to him and kissed her passionately, moving her toward the bed. They collapsed onto the soft mattress, and Jason felt his body sink into the silky sheets.

'Wow,' he murmured. 'This is really comfortable.'

'I know,' Sienna agreed, her voice sleepy.

'It's been a long day,' Jason said. His body ached from the fight, and he couldn't keep his eyes open.

'Yeah.' Sienna sounded far away.

I'm in bed with Sienna, Jason thought happily, just before he fell sound asleep.

Twelve

'We're late,' Sienna said the next day at lunchtime.

'I'm going as fast as I can. I don't have super-fast healing skills like some people,' Jason joked, making his way slowly through the hallway toward the school cafeteria. His body was still sore from last night's fight.

Sienna slowed to match him. 'Ugh, I'm so stressed,' she sighed. 'I know we all thought coming to school and acting normal was the right thing to do. But I can't think about anything except Christopher, the vampire who helped Van Dyke. Who knows what kind of experiments they could be doing on the poor guy right now.'

'I know.' Jason took her hand and squeezed. 'I think everyone is preoccupied. Adam hasn't made a single film reference all day!'

'Wow!' Sienna said with a tiny smile.

'Don't worry. We'll make a plan today and we'll rescue Christopher as soon as possible,' Jason assured her.

When they reached the cafeteria, the other vampires were all gathered around a big table in the back. Adam was on his way over, carrying a tray with a gigantic salad and a bottle of water.

'What, are you on a diet?' Jason teased him. 'Where's the pizza and Coke?'

Adam looked startled, but Sienna chuckled. 'Ignore him, Adam. Brianna probably convinced you to start eating healthy, right?'

'Um, yeah.' Adam blushed.

'Oh, I should've guessed,' Jason said. 'You guys must be pretty serious if you're letting her dictate your diet.'

'Well, I did have a taco for breakfast,' Adam defended himself. He plopped his tray onto the vampires' table and sat down. Jason and Sienna sat next to him.

'What's going on?' Sienna asked.

'Argument,' Belle told her. 'Van Dyke wants us to gather as many vampires as possible and then charge the warehouse because there's no way they could fight so many vampires at once. Zach thinks we need to sneak in and avoid another fight.'

'I'm with Zach,' Jason said. 'One fight against the freakishly strong humans was enough. And what if they called for reinforcements after last night?'

'Good point,' said Brad.

'Besides, I don't fight,' Belle put in. 'I believe in peace.'

'You just don't want to break a nail,' Van Dyke grumbled.

'I can kick your butt, Michael. Or don't you remember the locker incident from eighth grade?' Belle said sweetly.

Van Dyke flushed red, and Jason smiled. 'You'll have to tell me about that sometime,' he murmured to Sienna.

'Focus, people,' Brad commanded them. 'If we're sneaking in, that means we have to find an entrance that the security goons aren't watching.' He grabbed a pen from the table and began sketching on a napkin. 'The place was all one storey, with the lighted doorway here . . .' He drew a rough plan of the place as he talked. 'I thought I saw a bank of windows on this side—'

'But there were bars on them,' Zach put in. 'We can't get in that way.'

Brad drew little Xs over the window on his napkin blueprint.

'Let me see that pen,' Sienna said suddenly, grabbing it from him.

'Hey!' Brad protested.

Sienna ignored him. 'Where did you get this?'

'I borrowed it from Belle in English,' Brad said.

'I took it from the van last night,' Belle added. 'Why?'

'The logo looks really familiar to me,' Sienna said thoughtfully. 'Look.' She held the pen out so they could all see the logo: an H and a C intertwined in elaborate script.

'I don't recognize it,' Zach said.

'Me neither,' Jason admitted.

'Well, I do. And if it came from the van, it could give us some more information about what we're dealing with.' Sienna stood up. 'You guys keep planning. I'm going to take this to the computer room and see what I can dig up about the logo.' She gave Jason a quick kiss and took off.

Brad sighed. 'Anyone else have a pen I can borrow?'

'Don't worry about drawing the warehouse,' Adam said. 'I think I can get the actual blueprints for us.'

Everybody stared at him in surprise.

'Brianna's mom is a realtor,' Adam explained. 'And she just happens to cover commercial real estate in that area.'

'What are you saying?' Zach asked.

'Well, I mentioned the warehouse to Brianna this morning, and she says her mother brokered a deal for it last year. So I can get Brianna to look in the files, find out who bought it, and get us a copy of the schematics for the whole place.'

Brad let out a whistle. 'That would be great.'

'You can't tell Brianna why we need them, though,' Jason pointed out. 'How are you going to convince her to help?'

'I'll make up a story,' Adam said with a shrug. 'It'll be just like writing a movie script. Leave it to me.'

'Thanks, Adam,' Zach said. 'You're a good friend.' He turned to the rest of the group. 'Let's meet up at Van Dyke's place after school. Adam will bring the schematics, and we'll figure out the best way in.'

'Hey! Maybe we could tunnel in,' Van Dyke suggested. 'Like in that film, er . . . *The Great Gatsby.*'

He means The Great *Escape*, Jason thought, waiting for Adam to correct Van Dyke. But Adam didn't say anything. Jason guessed the situation was just too serious.

'Let's wait until we've seen the plans,' Zach said.

'OK,' Van Dyke agreed. 'But then those security guys better watch out, because I'm not leaving this time – not without Christopher.'

Sienna was waiting on her doorstep when Jason pulled up in the VW that evening. She'd changed out of the short skirt she wore to school, and now she had on a pair of jeans that hugged her curves and made his pulse pound. *I can't believe we fell asleep last night*, he thought ruefully. Was he ever going to get a chance to really *be* with his girlfriend?

'Thanks for the ride,' she said, climbing in next to him. 'The Spider started, but it was making that funny clanging sound.'

'That's never good.' Jason put the VW in gear and pulled back out onto the road. 'Did you find out anything about that logo on the pen?'

'Yup. Ten minutes of internet research and I had it. HemoCorp. That's what the H and the C stand for.'

'What's HemoCorp?' Jason asked.

'It's some kind of scientific think-tank. I must've seen the logo on papers in my dad's office or something. It's a subsidiary of Medi-Life, I think.'

'The big drug company?'

'Yeah, their headquarters are around here, off Mulholland Highway,' Sienna said. 'You don't think those security guys stole the van from Medi-Life, do you?'

'I think it's more likely that they stole the *pen*,' Jason said. 'But either way, we should get rid of that van as soon as possible. Because *we* definitely stole it, and even though Adam has connections with the police, I don't think we can get away with grand theft auto.'

'Let's search the van for evidence tonight, as soon as we get to Van Dyke's,' Sienna suggested. 'Then while the guys are breaking in to the warehouse tonight, the rest of us can get rid of the van somehow.'

'Sounds like a plan,' Jason replied. 'Although if there's any breaking and entering to be done, I'm going along.'

'Jason—' Sienna began.

'I'm going,' he insisted. 'I wasn't much help last night, but you never know when a spare set of fists can come in handy. I feel like I owe it to Van Dyke to help save Christopher.'

Sienna didn't look happy, but she nodded.

Jason turned the VW into Van Dyke's driveway, and they went inside. Everybody was gathered in the living room, waiting for Adam to arrive with the schematics.

'Sienna and I are going to check out the van some more,' Jason announced. 'See if Van Dyke's captors left anything behind that might give us a little information about what we're dealing with.'

'It's in the garage,' Van Dyke said. 'I meant to search it myself today, but I couldn't handle getting back inside that thing. I feel like I might explode if I don't get to Christopher soon.'

Brad laid a hand on his shoulder. 'We'll save him. Don't worry. As soon as Turnball gets here, we'll have a plan.'

Sienna led Jason through the kitchen and into Van Dyke's attached garage. Jason frowned when he saw the large dent in the side of the black van – the dent made by his body colliding with the metal. Whatever their plan was for tonight, he hoped it didn't involve a repeat of last night's brawl.

'You take the back, I'll take the front,' Sienna suggested.

Jason nodded and opened up the double doors at the back. Since it was a cargo van, it had no seats in back, just bare black floor mats. 'Shouldn't be too hard to search,' he said. 'Although I feel like I should be wearing gloves, just so I don't leave any evidence of myself behind.'

'This isn't *CSI*,' Sienna told him. 'Besides, we were all in this van last night. If there's evidence, there's evidence. I'm more interested in what those security goons left behind.'

Jason crawled around for ten minutes, pulling up the floor mats and peering at the dusty metal underneath, but he didn't find anything more interesting than a couple of paper clips and an old can of WD-40. He climbed out the back and went around to the driver's side door. 'I got nothing,' he reported.

'The cab is pretty clean, too,' Sienna said. 'There isn't even a registration in the glove compartment. But I did find this.' She handed him a small brown bottle.

'Looks like a prescription bottle,' he said.

'But there's no label,' Sienna pointed out. 'And there are no markings on the pills inside.'

Jason took off the cap and shook a couple of pills into his hand. They were dark red with no identifying marks. 'Are you sure they're not just mutant M&Ms?' he joked.

'You want to try one and find out?' Sienna challenged.

'Nope. Let's go show everyone else.' Jason pocketed the pills and helped Sienna out of the van, helping himself to a kiss along the way.

When they got back inside, the group had moved to the kitchen, where they were all studying a set of blueprints spread out on the table.

'Hey, Adam,' Jason said, surprised to see his friend there. Usually Adam would seek him out before just sitting right down with the vampire crew. But maybe he was as anxious to get down to business as the rest of them.

'Hi.' Adam shot him a smile. 'I got the plans, but we have to get them back to Brianna by tomorrow morning so she can sneak them back into the filing cabinet before her mother notices they've gone.'

'What did you tell Brianna?' Jason asked. 'Some elaborate conspiracy story?'

'Sort of,' Adam said.

'He probably told her he was researching a movie,' Belle said, giving Adam a nudge. 'Am I right?'

Adam grinned. 'You know me too well.'

'Does the file say who the warehouse was sold to?' Sienna asked.

'No, just that it was a private investor,' Adam replied. 'There wasn't even a name, just a bank account.'

'Well, you can hack into that and find out whose it is, can't you?' Zach asked.

'I tried, my man. The account was closed right after the sale last year,' Adam said. 'It's a dead end.'

Look at him getting all cosy with the vampires, Jason thought, amused. *I don't think anyone has ever called Zach Lafrenière 'my man' before.*

'Tear yourselves away from the plans for a minute,' Sienna told her friends. 'We found something in the van.'

Jason pulled out the bottle of pills and placed them on the table. 'No markings,' he said.

'But they were in the driver's seat. I think maybe they fell out of someone's pocket when they were driving,' Sienna said.

Zach frowned as he looked at the pills. 'We need to find out what these pills are,' he said. 'Sienna, can you take them to the DeVere Center and get the lab techs to analyze them? I know it's late but, given that your father practically owns the place, they should be willing to work all night if you ask them.'

'I'm on it,' Sienna said.

'I'll go with you.' Belle got up and grabbed her purse from the counter as Sienna bent to kiss Jason.

'Be careful,' Sienna whispered.

'You too,' he told her.

As she and Belle left, Van Dyke looked worried. 'Hang on, we're not waiting for the analysis before we make our rescue attempt, are we?'

'We probably should,' Zach said. 'But I'm starting to worry that Christopher may not have time for us to wait. You said he was in bad shape already, right?'

Van Dyke nodded. 'And that was two days ago,' he added.

'I say we go tonight,' Jason put in. 'We find a way in on the blueprints, and we go pull Christopher out.'

'You're going with them?' Adam cried, surprised.

'Um, yeah.' Jason raised an eyebrow. 'Aren't you?'

Adam's mouth fell open and his face paled. 'Uh . . . well . . .'

Everybody burst out laughing.

'Chill out, Turnball, nobody expects you to get involved with this,' Brad said.

'Well, *more* involved,' Erin put in.

'No, no, if I'm supposed to go, I'll go,' Adam said, his voice a mere squeak.

'Honestly, dude, I think you'd be a liability in a fight,' Van Dyke told him. 'I'd be so busy trying to protect you that I wouldn't be able to think straight.'

'I thought the point was to do this without another fight,' Maggie chided him.

'Yeah, and besides, I know how to punch,' Adam protested. 'I've seen lots of boxing movies.'

'That settles it, you're not coming,' Zach laughed. 'You can't risk getting caught breaking and entering, anyway, Adam. Your father would kill you. You've already helped us enough.'

'OK, OK, if you insist,' Adam replied in a relieved tone. 'Anyway, look, I was thinking this air vent might be the best way to go.' He pointed out a section on the north side of the warehouse schematic. 'This says the opening is two by three. Plenty of crawling room.'

'And it will take us right into the main warehouse,' Zach said. 'Good plan.'

'Let's get ready.' Brad jumped up, followed by Van Dyke.

'Erin and I will take the van out and dump it somewhere. I'm thinking long-term parking at the airport – that's what they did once on *The Sopranos*. Call if there's any trouble,' Maggie said. She hugged Van Dyke. 'Don't fight.'

'We'll see,' he said grimly.

'I'm gonna get these blueprints back to Brianna,' Adam said, rolling them up. 'Jason, walk me out?'

Jason nodded and followed Adam out to the driveway where his Vespa was parked. 'Listen, I wasn't kidding in there. Are you sure you want to go along with them?' Adam asked quietly. 'I saw that fight last night, Jason. Those guys might have *killed* you if we hadn't gotten you out of there. They meant business.'

'I know,' Jason said. 'And those are the guys holding Christopher hostage. That's why we've got to save him.'

'Agreed. But maybe you should just let the vampires handle this,' Adam argued. 'They can take the beatings and be better in an hour. You can't.'

'I appreciate the concern,' Jason said honestly. 'But they're my friends. I can't let them do this alone.'

'OK.' Adam climbed onto his Vespa. 'But Jason . . . don't say I didn't warn you.'

Thirteen

'What do you think?' Brad asked. They were hiding behind the same stand of trees as last night, and the warehouse looked just the same – except that now there was a guard standing under the pale yellow security light.

'Is that a gun?' Van Dyke asked.

'I don't think so.' Zach squinted into the darkness. 'It's definitely a weapon, though.'

'Guess we scared them last night,' Van Dyke said, 'even if we didn't hurt them.'

'I only see the one guard,' Jason put in. 'As long as he doesn't notice us, it should be fine.'

'Yeah, we've been watching for fifteen minutes. If they had anyone else patrolling, we would've seen them by now,' Zach said. 'Let's move.'

They moved stealthily down the hillside. Jason could hardly believe how silent the vampires' movements were. Watching Zach and Van Dyke ahead of him, he might almost have thought they were shadows.

When they reached the driveway, Zach stopped. He pointed to the right, where the small parking area curved around the warehouse. Between the building and the steep hillside there was only a space of about twenty feet.

Jason frowned. They had to circle around that way to get to the air vent. Unfortunately, that meant crossing directly in front of the guard.

'We have to take him out,' Brad whispered. 'There's no other way.'

'Adam says that when he's writing a screenplay, the simplest solution is usually the best,' Jason whispered.

'Meaning?' Zach asked.

'Oldest trick in the book,' Jason said. 'We throw something over to the left, the guard turns to check it out, and we run by on the right.'

'Seriously?' Even in a whisper, Jason could hear the doubt in Van Dyke's voice.

'It's worth a shot,' Jason said. 'If it doesn't work, we'll try to take him down before he raises the alarm. But that's risky.'

'I agree. I'll do it,' Zach said. He glanced around, then grabbed a sizeable tree branch lying on the ground. With a simple flick of his wrist, he sent it flying so far through the air that it crashed into the warehouse at the opposite end from where they were crouched.

The sound was loud in the silence. The guard jumped, then jogged over to check it out.

'Go, go, go!' Jason whispered frantically.

They all took off running, straight past the yellow-lit door and around the corner of the building to the right. Jason flattened himself against the wall and held his breath. Five seconds . . . ten seconds . . .

'Is he coming?' Brad's whisper was so low that Jason could barely hear him.

Zach, closest to the corner, inched along the wall until he was at the end. He listened for a moment, then shook his head. 'Let's get moving.'

They moved down the building, searching for the air vent. Finally Jason shook his head in frustration. 'We should've seen it already. We're almost to the end and the schematic showed the vent right in the middle of the north side.'

'I see it,' Brad replied suddenly.

They all turned to him in surprise.

'Look up,' he added.

Jason looked. Sure enough, there was a darker square in the dark wall – *fifteen feet up* in the dark wall.

'Huh,' Van Dyke said. 'I didn't notice that on the blueprints.'

'Whatever,' Zach replied. 'We'll just have to jump up.'

'Um, guys,' Jason told them. 'Not all of us can actually jump that high. Sorry.'

'Right,' Brad said. 'I'll give you a boost.' He shot Jason a teasing grin, and Jason rolled his eyes.

'You're just afraid to go first,' he joked, putting his foot into Brad's cupped hands. Brad's version of a boost practically catapulted Jason into the air. *Sometimes these vampires don't realize their own strength*, he thought. *Or maybe Brad's just messing with me.*

'There's a grate,' he called down as quietly as possible. 'Hold me steady.' He dug his fingers underneath the metal frame and tugged with all his strength. The grate gave way with a pop, and Jason pulled it all the way off. He handed it down to Zach, who put it on the ground silently.

Jason stuck his arms into the vent and pulled himself up and inside, crawling forward so that the vampires would have room to get in behind him. He heard Brad jump up to the edge and pull himself up, then Van Dyke. Zach brought up the rear.

Jason crawled forward as quickly as possible. It wasn't easy, as the vent was smaller than Adam had thought it would be, and Jason had to pull himself along combat-style on his stomach. He hoped he wasn't going too slowly for the vampires. They could probably combat crawl with superhuman speed, too. But nobody said anything and Jason decided not to worry about it. He'd been with these guys in bad situations before, and they'd never complained.

'We're here,' he whispered back when he saw another grate in the floor of the vent up ahead. There was some dim reddish light coming through it. Jason peered at the metal up close and realized that this grate was attached on the other side. 'Piece of cake,' he muttered, pushing it down. It popped out of the vent and began to fall into the room. Jason caught it by one corner to keep it from crashing onto the floor below. He pulled the grating up into the vent and put it on the other side of the hole.

Cautiously, Jason stuck his head down through the opening. The vent was attached to the ceiling in here, and the floor was lost in darkness below. The red light came from an 'Exit' sign hanging over a doorway in the wall to the far left. *Probably the door with the guard outside*, Jason thought.

Getting down wasn't going to be fun. The air vent was too narrow to turn around in, so Jason eased himself over to the other side of the opening on his stomach, then let his feet drop through. He scooted down until his body hung from the vent with only his arms and head still inside.

'It's a long drop,' he muttered.

'I'll lower you,' Brad said. He grabbed Jason by the wrists and leant through the opening, lowering Jason another few feet down. Jason took a deep breath, nodded at Brad, then dropped. He fell through the air for a moment, then hit the concrete floor – hard. But Jason was ready for it. He went immediately into a roll, then jumped to his feet. The fall had been jarring, but nothing was broken. Still, watching as Brad, Van Dyke and Zach jumped down and landed lightly on their feet, Jason couldn't help being a tiny bit jealous of their vampire super-abilities!

Zach glanced around. 'What a dump!' he murmured.

Jason took it in. The warehouse was mostly one big room, empty except for a few trolleys for moving stock around. The only light came from the 'Exit' sign and a few windows high up in the walls that let in some moonlight from outside. A dark doorway was cut into one wall.

'Does this look familiar?' Jason asked Van Dyke, keeping his voice low.

'No,' Van Dyke said shortly. 'But I know for sure that the guys here last night were the same guys that were holding me captive. I'd know that New Yorker's voice anywhere.'

'The place is empty, though,' Jason pointed out. 'You couldn't really hold prisoners in here. You said you were in a cell, right, Van Dyke?'

Van Dyke nodded.

'Then it can't have been in here,' Zach said. 'Let's see where that door goes.' He led the way over to the darkened doorway and stepped through. Jason and the others followed. The door led to a hallway that ran the length of the warehouse and ended in another outside door marked with an 'Exit' sign.

'It's a dead end,' Brad said, frustrated.

'No, it's not.' Jason felt a thrill of excitement run through him as he pointed to the floor five feet in front of him. 'There's a trap door.'

The other guys stared at it. 'Nice work, Freeman,' Zach said quietly. 'The cells must be underground.'

Jason stalked over and tugged on the steel handle. It didn't budge. He tried again. Nothing. 'It's bolted shut,' he said. 'We didn't bring any tools.'

'Back up,' Zach said. He grabbed the handle and jerked it straight up. The entire steel door flew up, its hinges busted. Zach put it down next to his feet.

'Oh, right, you don't need tools,' Jason said wryly.

'Stairs,' Van Dyke announced, peering into the hole. 'They look pretty rickety. Go slow.' He stepped down into the darkness, Brad following him. When it was

Jason's turn, he put his foot gently on the wooden step, feeling it give way a little bit under his weight. He got down about five steps before Zach climbed in behind him, pulling the trap door back over the opening to cover their tracks.

Jason climbed down another few steps in darkness. They had flashlights with them, but everyone had agreed they were only to be used in emergencies. Flashlights were a sure way of getting noticed in the dark.

'I hear something,' Brad's voice came softly from below.

Jason listened. 'Me too,' he whispered. 'Sort of a . . . buzzing noise.'

'Right. A hum,' Van Dyke put in. 'It's coming from the bottom.'

His voice sounded strange, but in the darkness Jason couldn't see Van Dyke's face to tell if he was all right. 'Do you . . . do you recognize that sound?' he asked.

'Yeah. I think so.' Van Dyke's voice shook.

'I can't see a thing,' Brad complained.

'I'm at the bottom,' Van Dyke replied in a loud whisper. 'There's light down here.'

Brad climbed down, then Jason. As he got lower, the ambient noise became louder. When he got to the bottom, he stopped to wait for Zach. He'd been expecting a basement cut out of the rock of the hillside, something dank and rough. But the walls here were smooth concrete. And, just like Van Dyke had said, there was light coming from further down the passageway. It flickered blue and white.

'The light's coming from round the corner,' Brad said. 'That's why it doesn't shine up here.'

'Go slowly,' Zach told them. 'If they built prisoner cells down here, there are probably guards. And the buzzing sound could be a security system.'

They inched up to the end of the concrete wall, then peered around the corner. Jason drew in a breath, shocked.

It wasn't a small hallway with a couple of rough-hewn cells. It was a wide, sanitary-looking white corridor with closed steel doors on either side, fluorescent tube lighting overhead, and polished linoleum floors. The hall stretched out so far in front of them that Jason couldn't even see the end of it. He did see another corridor intersecting with it about a hundred feet away, though. The place was huge.

'What the hell?' Van Dyke asked.

'It looks like an office building,' Brad said, confused.

'An office building out of some sort of Bond movie,' Jason replied. 'Adam should be here.'

'Does this look familiar?' Zach asked Van Dyke.

'No. They had me blindfolded a lot. But that noise . . .' Van Dyke shook his head and Jason could tell he was freaked out. He shook it off and peered around. 'This place looks big. I have no idea which way to go to find Christopher.'

'Then there's only one thing to do,' Zach said. 'Start here and look behind every door until we find him.'

'That could take hours,' Jason said. 'Should we split up?'

'Could be dangerous,' Brad replied.

'Let's stick together for now,' Zach decided. He stepped out into the white hallway and moved swiftly to the first door. He peered through the window in the door and turned back. 'That's just an office. Hopefully a lot of these doors will be like that and we can rule them out quickly.'

'Yeah, because when we find the prisoner cells, it will be obvious,' Van Dyke said grimly. 'Believe me, they weren't like this. I remember it being dark all the time.'

Jason glanced into the next door window. A desk, a filing cabinet and a white board on the wall. 'Another office.'

'This door has no window,' Brad said from ten feet further down the hall. 'And it's locked.'

'That shouldn't stop us,' Zach told him, reaching for

the door handle. Before he could even touch it, the handle jerked down and the door began to open. Zach sprang away, and they all sprinted back to the dark staircase they'd come from.

Jason threw himself against the wall, then inched out slowly until he could see down the white corridor. Two men had come out of the door and were busy locking it again. They both wore crisp white lab coats, and one of them carried a clipboard. When the door was locked, they headed down the hall without even a glance toward the hall with the staircase. Jason watched until they turned left down the other hallway.

'They're gone,' Jason reported to his friends. 'They were dressed like lab technicians.'

'Maybe they were the ones doing experiments on me,' Van Dyke growled.

'Let's find Christopher.' Brad stepped back out in the corridor and they all moved quickly to the locked steel door. With a quick jerk on the handle, Brad broke the lock and pulled the door open. Inside was an examination table and a stainless steel counter, but no vampire prisoner.

'Keep moving,' Zach said. He led them back out into the corridor. The next door was on the other side of the hallway – another empty exam room. Zach went to the next door and reached for the handle. As Jason walked over to check out the one opposite, a tinny-sounding voice crackled through the air, gradually getting louder as if it was moving towards him.

'. . . eye out for intruders,' it was saying. 'Four males, possibly dangerous.'

'That's a walkie-talkie,' Jason whispered frantically to his friends. 'They know we're here!'

As he spoke, he became aware of the sound of approaching footsteps – footsteps moving in unison, as if an army unit were marching toward him.

'In here!' Zach called, yanking open his door and frantically gesturing them inside. Jason rushed in with Brad and Van Dyke, and Zach pulled the door closed behind them.

'You're stepping on my foot,' Brad complained to Van Dyke.

'Give me a break, man, this is just like a storage closet or something. There's no room,' Van Dyke grumbled.

'Quiet!' Zach hissed. He eased the door open a tiny crack, and Jason could see a sliver of the corridor. The marching feet were practically on top of them now. Jason spotted a guy dressed in black, a nasty looking crossbow clutched in his hands. Another man followed, and another, all armed with crossbows.

'Check the warehouse,' a deep voice ordered. The

three crossbow guards kept going, headed for the staircase, while a fourth big guy stepped into Jason's line of sight and stopped. He rested his crossbow on his shoulder and pulled out a walkie-talkie. 'No sightings in the office wing, Mr Norton,' he said into the walkie, his deep voice echoing in the hallway, 'but we're checking upstairs and expect to apprehend the intruders soon.'

The walkie-talkie gave a beep and another voice crackled through. 'Keep me posted.'

'Roger.' The guard holstered his walkie-talkie, gripped his crossbow, and marched off after the others.

'We must've tripped an alarm when we opened the trap door,' Zach said. 'Dammit!'

'They have crossbows,' Jason added, the memory of Tamburo's crossbow bolt flying toward him filling his mind. 'They're prepared for vampires.'

'So they know we're here, and they know what we are,' Brad said, fear creeping into his voice.

Jason nodded, trying to ignore the growing pit of terror in his own stomach. 'You guys? They have scientists, cells and guards with crossbows . . . What the hell kind of place is this?'

Fourteen

'Whatever it is. We have to move, and fast,' Zach said. 'Those guards went upstairs to search the warehouse for us, which means they'll be back.'

'That place is so empty, it will only take them two minutes to see that we're not there,' Van Dyke agreed.

'There are only two doors on this hallway we haven't checked,' Jason said. 'Then we hit an intersection with another hall.'

'Brad and I will check the door on the right,' Zach said. 'Jason and Van Dyke, get the one on the left. Then we'll turn down the new hallway to put some distance between ourselves and those guards.'

'The lab coat guys went to the left,' Jason told him.

'Then we'll follow them,' Zach said. 'Let's move.'

He shoved open the door and they all took off at a run. Van Dyke reached the last door on the left, listened for a moment to see if there was anyone inside, then grabbed the handle and pulled. Jason threw himself into the room and took a quick look around. Stainless steel counters, an empty examination table and some lightboards on the wall.

'Nothing here. Let's go,' he said, pushing past Van Dyke into the hallway.

Across the hall, Zach and Brad were exiting another door. Zach met Jason's eye and shook his head.

Without breaking stride, Jason took off for the other hallway, the three vampires right behind him. He rounded the corner at a jog and glanced around. The fluorescent lights here had a weird lavender tinge to them, but otherwise the corridor was identical to the last one – white floors and walls and a series of unmarked steel doors.

Jason rushed forward, heading for the first door. But suddenly a high-pitched shriek split the air, pulsing in a way that made Jason's head throb. There was something else in the noise, too, some kind of odd tone that made him instantly nauseous. He spun around to see Zach, Brad, and Van Dyke a few steps behind him, holding their ears in pain. All three of them were doubled over, and it was obvious that they were in much worse shape than Jason.

Super-hearing equals super-painful, Jason realized. *And that weird sound is obviously meant to hurt vampires.*

He started back toward his friends just as the

shrieking sound changed to a strange metallic clang.

Jason stopped in his tracks and looked up.

The ceiling was moving. *Collapsing.*

'Look out!' Zach yelled.

Jason leapt back just as a thick steel plate dropped from the ceiling like the blade of a guillotine. He fell onto his back, gasping in shock and relief. The thing had fallen less than an inch in front of him.

Jason scrambled to his feet and stared. Where his friends had stood two seconds ago was only a blank metal wall. For a split second, his brain couldn't compute what had just happened. Then he hurled himself at the wall, pounding on it with his fists.

'Zach! Brad!' he yelled. 'Van Dyke!'

Dimly, he heard pounding on the other side. 'Freeman!' Zach called, his voice muffled by the steel door. 'We're trapped in here. There are walls on both sides.'

'I'm still free,' Jason called. 'How can I help?'

'It's all steel,' Brad answered. 'There's no way out.'

'Run, Freeman!' Zach yelled. 'You have to find Christopher.'

The high-pitched alarm was still blaring, and Jason felt his heart pounding along with it. The guards would be here any second, obviously. Jason turned and sprinted down the hall. He couldn't get caught. He was Christopher's only hope now.

I'm everybody's *only hope now*, a voice in his head whispered. Somehow, he had to find a way to rescue Christopher – and all of his friends.

'Think, Jason,' he ordered himself. He absolutely could not afford to be found. Which meant he needed to fit in here. Which meant . . . what?

Jason reached a doorway and grabbed the handle. Locked. He raced to the next one . . . it was open! He slipped inside the room and pulled the door shut. A quick scan of the room told him it was another office. Filing cabinet, desk, chair, lab coat . . . Lab coat! As soon as Jason saw the coat draped over the back of the chair, he knew what to do. Running through a secret underground facility looking like an intruder wasn't going to work.

But walking confidently down the hallway dressed as if he worked here? Well, it was worth a shot.

He snatched the lab coat and slipped it on, glancing at the ID tag clipped to the pocket. 'Bill Baldwin, hope you don't mind,' he muttered. Then he frowned, looking more closely. In the corner of the ID tag was a small logo – an H and a C, intertwined. 'HemoCorp,' Jason said, surprised. 'Guess that pen in the van wasn't stolen, after all.'

He opened the door and stepped back out into the hallway, then walked as fast as possible away from the steel wall holding his friends, his head spinning. HemoCorp ... this place belonged to HemoCorp. What had Sienna said about that company – that it was a think-tank?

He came to another intersection of corridors. Without stopping, he turned left, his mind still on HemoCorp.

It doesn't make sense, Jason thought. *Why would a think-tank have a bunch of underground offices? Why would they have giant steel doors that drop from the ceiling? Why would they kidnap and experiment on vampires?*

'I think they're a subsidiary of Medi-Life...' Sienna's voice rang in his memory.

Jason kept walking, forcing himself to think. Medi-Life was a drug company, one of the biggest and most successful. This place was huge and secret and filled with laboratory rooms, all with an obviously expensive security system. The guys guarding it were humans who seemed to have vampire strength. And in the van they'd found a pen from HemoCorp, a part of Medi-Life.

And a bottle of pills, Jason remembered suddenly. What did those pills have to do with it all? Could this entire place be funded by Medi-Life?

All of a sudden, Jason felt a surge of fear so

overwhelming that he stopped walking. Stopped even thinking. This was bigger than Van Dyke or Christopher. It was bigger than some human guys who were freakishly strong. Zach, Brad and Van Dyke hadn't just been captured by some little operation with a vendetta against vampires. They'd been taken by a huge company with seemingly unlimited resources. A company that was experimenting on vampires . . . and Jason had no idea why. But the ideas that ran through his head weren't comforting.

'Do you know what's going on?' A voice broke into Jason's thoughts.

'I heard there was some kind of break-in.' Two women in lab coats were walking toward him, speaking in hushed voices.

Jason began walking again, trying to shake off his fears. He couldn't get caught, so he had to get past these workers without arousing suspicion. He kept his eyes on the ground and walked quickly down the hall, not even glancing in their direction.

The women passed him and disappeared around the corner, and Jason breathed a sigh of relief.

He forced himself to focus. The main thing right now was to find Christopher and get him out of here. Freaking out about who was behind it all wasn't going to help anybody. For the first time, Jason took a good look around and realized that this corridor wasn't the same as the others he'd been in. This one was narrower, darker, *older*. The lights overhead were dim, and the steel doors in the wall were solid, with no windows.

The hallway felt damp, more like a basement than like the scientific labyrinth he'd been in. *Van Dyke said his cell felt cold and damp, like a warehouse*, Jason remembered. Maybe he'd looped back around under the warehouse again.

Tap, tap, tap.

Jason frowned, listening. The sound was muffled, like a hammer tapping in an underground mine.

Bang, bang, bang.

It was louder now, a little, but Jason still couldn't tell where the sound was coming from. He glanced behind him. The narrow hallway was empty.

Tap, tap, tap.

Jason hesitated, then kept walking forward. It looked as if the hall ended about fifty feet away. The hammering sound was probably just the HemoCorp people – or the Medi-Life people – doing construction on their big underground lab. Other than this hallway, everything in the place screamed 'new'.

Tap, tap, tap. Bang, bang, bang! Tap, tap, tap.

Jason stopped. That didn't really sound like

construction hammering. It sounded like a pattern – a familiar pattern.

Tap, tap, tap. Bang, bang, bang! Tap, tap, tap.

'It can't be,' Jason gasped.

Tap, tap, tap. Bang, bang, bang! Tap, tap, tap.

It was – he was sure of it – Morse Code. Just like Adam had shown him at Brad's party. Three dots, three dashes, three dots: SOS. Somebody was asking for help!

Jason veered over to the nearest steel door. He pulled on it, but it was locked. He pressed his ear against the cold metal, and waited.

Tap, tap, tap. Bang, bang, bang! Tap, tap, tap.

The sound wasn't coming from this door. Jason moved to the next one, and listened. Then the next.

Tap, tap, tap. Bang, bang, bang! Tap, tap, tap.

This time, the banging was louder, and Jason thought he could feel the tiniest reverberation in the steel of the door. He pulled on it. Locked.

'Christopher?' he called.

Silence.

'Were you banging on the door?' Jason asked.

'There's nothing you can do to me, you know. I saw *Old Boy*, so I'm down with all the torture methods you can come up with!' a voice called from inside.

Jason gaped at the closed door. That wasn't Christopher. It couldn't be – because it was Adam.

That's impossible, Jason thought. *How did they get a hold of him?* Suddenly a bolt of fear shot through him. If these people had grabbed Adam, did that mean they were going after all of Jason's friends? Could they have Sienna, too?

'Adam!' Jason yelled. 'Are you alone in there?'

'Jason?' Adam's voice called. 'Is that you? I'm alone.'

'Hang on.' Jason grabbed the door handle again and pulled with all his strength. It didn't budge. Forcing himself to calm down, he studied the door. It was thick, and made of steel, and there was no way he could kick it down. He doubted even the vampires, with their super-strength, could knock out a door like this.

A tiny, flashing light caught Jason's eye. Set into the wall next to the door was a small sensor pad. It had two lights, red and green. And the red light was flashing.

'It can't be that easy,' Jason said. He glanced down at the ID badge on his stolen lab coat. Jason flipped the badge over. There was a magnetic strip along the back. 'Bill Baldwin, let's hope you have high-security clearance.' He pressed the magnetic strip to the sensor pad on the wall.

The light switched from red to green, and the heavy door gave out a distinctive *click*.

Before Jason could even move, Adam shoved the

door open and leapt out into the hallway. He threw his arms around Jason.

'I knew you'd come!' he cried. 'I heard people talking about intruders in the hallway, and I figured it had to be you. No one else would be crazy enough to try to infiltrate a place like this!'

Jason slapped his friend on the back and released him. 'Glad I could help,' he said, smiling. 'Although I wasn't actually here for you.' He studied Adam's face. The dude looked even paler than usual, and he was obviously shaken up, in spite of his joking behavior. 'You OK? I'm glad I was able to get you out so fast. How did they catch you?'

'I was on my way to Brianna's friend's place, and she's down in one of those winding canyons, you know? So all of a sudden, I see a tree branch down over the road. Which is weird, because it hasn't rained in months and there's no wind or anything. But whatever, the branch is blocking the road. So I get out to move it, and somebody jumps me from behind.'

Jason just stared at him. 'Huh?' he asked.

'I know,' Adam said. 'What do they want with me? Listen, how long have I been here? Is Brianna OK?'

Jason frowned. 'Wait. Why were you going to Brianna's friend's house? I thought you were heading back to her mother's office with the blueprints.'

Now Adam stared at Jason. 'What blueprints?'

'The schematics. For the warehouse,' Jason said. 'Or were you meeting Brianna at her friend's?'

'No, I was going to pick her up, remember?' Adam replied. 'For the barbecue at Van Dyke's place.'

'What?' Jason felt as if his brain was filled with cotton. He simply could not understand a thing his best friend was saying. 'The barbecue was two days ago. What are you talking about?'

'Two days!' Adam cried. 'I knew it had been a while, but I didn't think it was that long.'

'*What?*' Jason asked again.

'I mean, not like in the time-flies-when-you're-having-fun sense,' Adam corrected himself. 'Because I've totally not been having fun. But they've been decent to me – they keep feeding me and all. And nobody's taken me out to experiment on me, or torture me, or whatever. The guy in the next cell . . . well, it's bad. He's just whimpering constantly, like a dog with a broken leg. He's in real pain. They came a few hours ago, I think it was, and took him away somewhere. And when they opened his door I heard him screaming like he was terrified.' Adam's expression was more serious than Jason had ever seen it. 'It's horrible, Jason. We have to do something.'

Somewhere in the back of Jason's mind, he

registered what Adam was saying. A prisoner, being experimented on, in pain: it had to be Christopher.

But Jason still couldn't quite understand what Adam was talking about when he said he'd been here for two days. Or at least, his brain couldn't understand how to compute what Adam was saying. Because it would mean . . . it would mean . . .

'Are you saying that you've been locked in here since the day of Van Dyke's barbecue?' Jason asked. 'You don't know anything that's happened since then?'

'No. I mean yes. And no,' Adam said. 'I've definitely been here since the barbecue day. Why? What's happened?'

But other thoughts were rushing through Jason's head now. Bad thoughts. Terrifying thoughts. 'Adam,' he said. 'If you've been here for two days, then who gave us the blueprints for this building? Who helped us plan how to get in? And just who the hell has been with us in Malibu, pretending to be *you*?'

Fifteen

'What?' Adam cried. 'I'm sorry . . . *what?*'

'I said goodbye to you less than two hours ago. You were going to return the blueprints,' Jason told his best friend. 'It was *you.*'

'It was not,' Adam said firmly. Then he gasped. 'The vampire drugs! Someone must have taken the vampire drugs and changed his appearance to look like me.'

'You've lost me,' Jason told him.

'Vampires can change their appearance at will,' Adam explained. 'They can look like anyone they choose!'

'I know *that*,' Jason replied. 'I meant the "vampire drugs" – what the hell are you talking about?'

'Look, the guy in the cell next to me, the one they've been hurting?' Adam said quickly. 'He's been here a long time. When I first got here, he told me what he knew.'

'Through the walls?' Jason asked.

'The doors are steel, the walls are just . . . whatever

walls are made of,' Adam told him. 'Anyway, this guy – I think he's a vampire.'

'His name is Christopher,' Jason said. 'He's the one I'm here to save.'

'I thought you were here to save *me*?' Adam protested.

'I didn't know you were here, remember?' Jason said. 'I've been hanging out with Fake You for the last two days.'

'Oh. Right. Remind me to be offended by that later,' Adam replied. 'Anyway, so Christopher told me that this whole place is run by a man named Charles Norton. I don't know who he is, but apparently he was doing research or something in New York and he discovered the existence of vampires.'

'New York is where the vampire kidnappings started,' Jason said thoughtfully.

'O-kay. Now you've lost me,' Adam said. 'But, whatever. The point is, this guy Norton started experimenting on vampires to see what made them so cool. He wanted to figure out how to make humans have vampire skills – you know, the strength, the appearance changing, the super-healing.'

'It sounds like he found a way,' Jason said grimly.

'Christopher said that Norton had discovered enough about vampire genetics to formulate some short-term drugs. You know, shoot up and act like a vampire for two hours or something like that.' Adam shook his head. 'It's bad, Jason. If the way they were treating Christopher is any indication, I don't think Norton cares much about how he gets his vampire genetic info.'

'He experimented on Van Dyke, too,' Jason said.

Adam's jaw clenched. 'He all right?'

'He is now,' Jason told him. 'But all the adult vampires are off figuring out what to do about the New York situation. Nobody knew that Malibu was next on the list.'

'Christopher asked if we were in Malibu. They brought him from New York,' Adam confirmed. 'He said Norton told him the Malibu vampires were from a purer bloodline, that they were going to be better specimens for study.'

'It's true,' Jason said. 'Norton probably thinks that the purer blood will make his drugs stronger, too. But how could he possibly know that about the vampire bloodlines? I didn't even know it for a long time, and my own girlfriend is a vampire.'

Adam bit his lip. 'He, um, he has a source. A vampire. Somebody high up. Somebody who betrayed them all. That's what Christopher said.'

Jason's eyes widened in surprise. A *vampire* was involved with this?

'Who?' he demanded.

'I don't know. They came and took Christopher away after that. And when they brought him back, he just moaned the whole time,' Adam said sadly. 'He never said another word to me. I'm not sure he can even talk anymore.'

Jason ran his hand through his hair, frustrated. 'I can't believe this. We thought we had it under control. We thought it was a small operation, and we'd found their warehouse, and we were going to break in, rescue Christopher, and get back out. We thought there were six guys who were strong, but that's it. And now it turns out it's some evil guy from New York in league with a high-up vampire – and Medi-Life!'

'Medi-Life?' Adam asked.

'They own this place.' Jason handed over the ID badge for Adam to look at. 'And this Norton guy has been onto us all along. He even sent somebody to spy on us! Whoever it was pretending to be you was feeding us information, and we just believed him! We haven't been in control once, not even for a second. And now they've got Brad, Van Dyke and Zach.'

'OK, chill,' Adam said. 'We can be mad at ourselves later. Well, not so much me, because I didn't know about any of this and I didn't believe that some freaky impostor was my best friend, but—'

'You're right,' Jason interrupted. 'Now isn't the time to beat ourselves up about this. We'll figure out the big picture once we get out of this place – *with* our friends and Christopher.'

'Good. How?'

Jason thought about it. 'We can't go back out the way we got in, because Adam – Fake Adam – knows about that. In fact, he's the one who pointed out the air vent to us.'

'So he'll have goons waiting right outside the vent for us,' Adam reasoned.

'Besides, the way back is blocked by the giant steel doors that appeared out of the ceiling and trapped the vampires,' Jason said.

Adam whistled. 'That's some serious security.'

'Right. It's going to be tough,' Jason said. 'But we can't just stand here talking. Let's try to find Christopher.'

'They took him that way,' Adam said, pointing down the hall the way Jason had come. 'I heard them.'

Jason led the way back to the intersection with the next hallway. 'The rooms to the right were all empty, or else they were just offices,' he said. 'We'll go left.'

'Coming through,' somebody called, and a motorized cart went whizzing by, loaded down with gleaming silver lab equipment. The woman driving it barely even glanced at them as she passed.

Jason's heart gave a violent *thump* of surprise. He'd seen so few people down here that it was a shock to come across anybody at all.

'So if she thought we were intruders, she would have yelled at us, right?' Adam whispered, clearly as startled as Jason was.

'Right,' Jason said. 'She probably saw my lab coat and figured I work here, then didn't think any more about it.'

'I need to get a lab coat, too,' Adam said. 'Just to be safe, you know?'

There was a door five feet away. Jason tried it – locked. He waved the ID card over the sensor pad on the wall, and the door clicked open.

'See? I need one of those . . .' Adam's voice trailed off as he got a look at what was inside the room. It was a laboratory. Not the kind of bland exam room Jason had seen in the other corridors, but a real, functioning lab with all kinds of beeping, whirring, scary-looking technology. And in the center of it all was a small tank filled with clear liquid . . . and an arm.

'Is that . . . is that a person?' Adam choked.

'It's part of a person,' Jason said, feeling sick.

'Oh my God, oh my God!' Adam turned away and stepped back into the hall. 'We have to get out of here.'

'Yeah,' Jason said grimly. '*All* of us.' He strode down

the corridor. The doors were farther apart here, probably because the labs were huge. At least that one lab had been. Jason passed his ID card over the sensor and the next door clicked open.

He and Adam went inside. Another lab, more busy-looking machines. But this one didn't have any tanks or horrible stuff. What it had was a dude in a head-to-toe suit like an astronaut. He was moving a strange-looking purple disk from one scanner to another, holding it with a pair of tongs.

'Let's go!' Jason hissed, shoving Adam out of the room before the guy could see them.

'What are they *doing* here?' Adam asked. 'This is like something out of an old *X-Files* episode.'

A maintenance man in a dark blue jumpsuit was mopping the floor of the hallway in front of them. Jason felt his pulse speed up as he walked toward the guy. Could they really just open up another laboratory door right in front of someone who worked here?

They had no choice but to try. At the next door, Jason confidently swiped his ID card at the sensor pad.

Nothing happened. Adam shot him a panicked look.

Jason tried again, but it was no use. Clearly this was one room that Bill Baldwin didn't have access to. And that meant it was higher security than the other labs.

Higher even than the prisoner cells. Something important was inside – or some*one*.

'We have to get in here,' Jason muttered. Summoning all his courage, he turned to the maintenance man. 'Hey! You have a pass card for all the rooms, right?'

The guy leant on his mop and rolled his eyes. 'They all gotta get clean.'

'Good. Let us into this lab,' Jason ordered, trying to sound like some kind of snobby research assistant. 'I accidentally demagnetized my card in Lab Two this morning.'

The maintenance man raised his eyebrows skeptically. 'I don't think so.'

'Look, my man. It's vital that we get into this laboratory, *right now*!' Adam said, stepping out from behind Jason.

The maintenance guy had a stubborn look in his eyes as he switched his gaze to Adam, but when he saw Jason's friend his eyes widened, he dropped the mop, and he hurried over with his pass card. 'Right away,' he said, swiping it over the sensor pad. The door clicked open.

'Thank you,' Adam said. 'Really.'

'Of course, sir,' the maintenance guy replied, shuffling back over to his mop and pail.

Jason pulled the door shut behind them, frowning. 'What was all that about?' he asked.

'He's a man of the people,' Adam said with a shrug. 'I figured we could appeal to his human side.'

But Jason was barely listening anymore, because there, hanging right in front of him, was the perfect disguise. The absolute *best* way not to get caught in this place was not to be *seen* in this place.

'You still want a lab coat, or do you want one of those?' he asked Adam, nodding toward the humungous astronaut suits on the wall.

Adam gasped. 'Oh, I want one of those!'

Jason glanced at the wall, where a sign labeled the suits 'CLEAN SUITS'. He pulled one of the heavy outfits down and handed it to Adam, then grabbed another for himself.

'What do you think they're supposed to keep us clean from?' Adam asked as they struggled to get in to the things.

'Who knows? Maybe they're supposed to keep the room clean from us,' Jason said. 'So we don't contaminate the experiments. I mean, look around. We're in an airlock.'

Adam glanced around the small anteroom. Sliding doors made of thick glass separated them from the main laboratory. 'OK. So boots and masks on,' he said, reaching for a pair of giant boots from the line along the wall. Jason took a helmet off a hook, then got one for Adam, too.

Once they were all suited up, Jason took a good look at his friend. Adam's entire body was covered by the suit. Even his head was completely covered, with only a small window showing his face. 'No one will know we don't belong,' Jason said into the intercom mike inside his helmet. 'I can barely even see you.'

Adam gave him a thumbs-up, then turned to the glass door. Jason found himself holding his breath as the door slowly slid open. What would they find inside? Christopher? Their friends? He just hoped it wasn't anything horrible.

The lab was eerily quiet inside. Most of the big machines were dark, and only one dim light shone in the room, illuminating an incubator tank.

Jason's stomach lurched. This tank was five times the size of the one in the other lab, the one with the arm. This one was big enough to hold an entire body.

Steeling himself, Jason moved over to the tank and peered down.

Beautiful, he thought. The guy inside the tank was a perfect-looking person, so impossibly beautiful that he resembled some artist's rendering of an angel more than a regular human being.

'A vampire,' he said shortly. 'In his natural state. That's the only time they're so good-looking. Usually they tone it down to fit in amongst us humans.'

'This is nobody's natural state,' Adam muttered from beside him.

Jason nodded. Besides his perfect physical appearance, the vampire was in bad shape. His eyes were open, but there was no sign of life in them. The pupils were so tiny that it was hard to see them at all. His mouth hung open, slack. And out of every single limb came a tube that snaked through the tank and connected to a huge machine at the vampire's feet. There was another tube in his mouth, one in his navel, and one more coming from the back of his neck.

Was this Christopher? Could they save him? It was hard to tell if he was even still alive.

'What are the tubes doing?' Jason asked.

'I don't know,' Adam replied. 'Nothing's moving right now. I can't see if the tubes are doing anything at all.'

'Do you think we can disconnect him?'

Adam shrugged. 'They did it in *The Matrix*.'

'OK.' Jason reached forward and took hold of the tube leading to the vampire's right hand. He hesitated. Should he just pull? He didn't want to hurt the guy even more . . .

'What are you doing?' a harsh voice broke his concentration. Jason jumped, and turned to see a middle-aged man, wearing a lab coat, staring at him from behind the glass door.

Adam turned his head toward Jason, and Jason could make out his friend's panicked expression even through the tiny window in the hood.

'Why are you wearing clean suits?' the man went on. 'The warning light is off.' He pointed to the top of the glass door, and for the first time, Jason noticed the light on the wall. Sure enough, it was off.

Oh my God, Jason thought, his blood running cold. *We screwed up. These stupid suits were supposed to disguise us, but instead they're going to give us away!*

'We're not conducting any level eight tests at the moment,' the man went on, his voice growing angry. 'So what the hell are you doing in here?'

Sixteen

Jason thought fast. 'My colleague and I were just about to commence level eight testing,' he lied, trying to sound authoritative. 'We were about to put the warning light on when I heard a noise coming from the ... subject. We came over to check on him.'

Please let me sound like I know what I'm talking about, Jason prayed silently.

The man in the lab coat studied him for a moment, then nodded.

Adam, eyes wide, turned back to the vampire and reached for the tube going into his stomach.

'Leave that one for now,' the man behind the glass said. 'I need your help with the new subjects.' He opened the sliding door, and a guy in a clean suit pushed a gurney into the room. On the gurney was another incubator tank – and inside the tank was Zach.

Jason already knew what was coming when he saw the other tanks wheeled in. Brad and Van Dyke were trapped helplessly in the tanks, strapped at the wrists and ankles and looking dazed. Even Zach, in his tank, seemed really out of it. All three of them had IV lines in their arms, and tubes in their mouths. The incubator tanks were closed, and inside there was a strange fog, as if a cloud were trapped within the glass.

Gas, Jason realized. Van Dyke had said they'd used some kind of gas to keep him sedated when he was here last time.

'They're still conscious, Dr Abell,' one of the clean-suit guys said.

The man behind the glass nodded. 'Get started with the wiring while I suit up.' He turned away and pulled a clean suit off the wall while two guys moved toward Van Dyke's tank. The third one headed for Brad. 'You two take that one,' he said, nodding Jason and Adam toward Zach.

For a moment, Jason felt paralyzed. These people expected him to help stick tubes into his friend! Blind fury raced through him, and his hands clenched into fists.

Adam moved over to the side of Zach's tank and turned so that Jason could see his face, eyebrows raised in a silent question. Jason knew what the question was: should they do something? Should they try to help their friends?

Every muscle in Jason's body was tensed and ready

to fight. But there were three guys in here, not to mention Dr Abell in the airlock. Even if he and Adam could take all of them alone, somebody was sure to set off an alarm. And the vampires were completely incapacitated. Who even knew if they'd be able to walk, let alone fight?

He shook his head at Adam. Then he picked up a coil of plastic tubing from one of the stainless steel counters. He watched as the other lab assistants straightened the tubing, and tried to copy them. He didn't know how they'd be able to play along when it came to actually inserting tubes into his friends' bodies, but right now he couldn't think more than a minute ahead.

Adam took a coil of tubing and began prepping it as well. Jason thought he looked a little green through the window in his hood, but he was hanging in there.

Casually, Jason moved to stand directly over Zach's head. He leant in enough for Zach to be able to see his face through the tiny window in his hood, then gave him what he hoped was a reassuring look. Zach blinked, then blinked again, as if he was trying to see more clearly.

He's pretty out of it, Jason thought. *I hope he could tell it was me.*

'Chop, chop!' Dr Abell barked, coming in from the

airlock in his clean suit. 'What's taking so long?' He moved to the guy at Brad's tank and snatched the tubing away from him. 'We've got to get them wired before—'

An insistent beeping interrupted him, and all the lab assistants turned toward the back wall. Baffled, Jason turned, too.

Half the wall was taken up by a huge flat-screen monitor, which had suddenly come to life. And on the monitor, larger than life, was Adam.

'Dr Abell, I see you have the intruders,' Fake Adam said in a vague New York accent.

There was a crash as Adam dropped the coil of tube he was holding. He turned away to pick it up, clearly trying to cover his shock at seeing his own face on the monitor.

Jason was a little shocked himself. It was obviously a communications device, and this was obviously the fake Adam that he'd been hanging out with for the last couple of days. And even now, knowing the guy was a fake, he couldn't tell the difference in their faces. The resemblance was exact.

'Yes, sir, Mr Norton,' Dr Abell said. 'Three vampires, just like you told us to expect.'

Jason turned to Adam, who was busy re-coiling the tubing, his back to the monitor. Jason went over to help him.

'Norton,' Adam said quietly, the helmet of his clean suit right next to Jason's. 'The guy in charge – *that's* who is impersonating me.'

'That's who has been hanging out with us for the last two days, setting us up to get caught,' Jason agreed.

'Very good,' Norton-Adam said. 'I'm in the car now. I expect them to be ready by the time I get back to the complex.'

'Yes, sir. As soon as they're wired, it shouldn't take long to put them into light comas,' Dr Abell replied. 'The last subject was comatose within five minutes.'

'Well, these vampires are stronger,' Norton-Adam said. 'Their blood is purer. I want you to take good care of them, Abell. Monitor the IV feeding constantly. The healthier we can keep them, the better the output will be.'

'Output?' Adam whispered.

'Of course, Mr Norton,' Dr Abell replied. 'The feeding tubes will allow for optimal output of blood, bone marrow and spinal fluid. But I'm afraid that the tissue will eventually suffer if they're kept comatose—'

'I'm not an idiot, Abell,' Norton-Adam snapped. 'We'll harvest the tissue first, while it's healthy, then take the fluids. We can wake them up in between harvests and let them move around to rebuild muscle tissue. Any bed sores will heal as soon as we let them regain their powers.'

'Perhaps a rotating schedule would work,' Dr Abell said. 'Since we have multiple subjects now, we can have one or two being harvested while the other one is recuperating.'

'Excellent idea,' Norton-Adam replied. 'We don't know how long it will be before we can isolate the vampiric DNA strands for replication. We may need to keep using their actual fluids and tissues for quite some time to make the drugs.'

'I'll work up a schedule immediately,' Dr Abell said, sounding very pleased with himself.

'Now, what about the human?' Norton-Adam asked.

Adam and Jason exchanged a worried look.

'Adam Turnball?' Dr Abell asked.

'No! Jason Freeman,' Norton-Adam answered. 'He broke in with the three vampires. I told security to take him to a cell.'

'I . . . they only apprehended the three vampire subjects,' Dr Abell said.

Jason shot a look over his shoulder at Norton-Adam. The guy looked seriously pissed off. 'You're telling me there's an *intruder* on the loose inside the complex?'

Dr Abell just shrugged helplessly.

'Unacceptable!' Norton-Adam snapped. Then he

seemed to calm down. 'Well, at least he's only a human.' A slow, self-satisfied grin worked its way across his face. 'Besides, if Freeman tries to cause any kind of trouble, I have just the thing to keep him in line.'

Jason's heart seemed to skip a beat. What did Norton mean by that? What did he think would keep Jason 'in line'?

Sienna. The thought was instantaneous. Norton – as Adam – had seen enough of Jason and Sienna over the past few days to realize how deep their relationship went. Did he have Sienna? Had he taken her hostage, too? Jason stared at the face on the monitor, anger fighting with terror in his mind.

'But, Abell, I want him found,' Norton-Adam was saying. '*Now.*'

'Yes, sir.'

'If he's not in custody by the time I get there, I will be very unhappy. Do you understand?' Norton-Adam's voice had taken on a deadly edge, and Jason could see that Dr Abell was frightened.

'Yes. Yes, sir. I'll—' Dr Abell began. But Norton-Adam was gone.

They all stared at the blank monitor for a moment. Then Dr Abell snapped back into command. 'You heard him! Find that boy!'

The clean-suit guys all scrambled for the door.

'He's probably going for the prisoner cells, thinking we'd put the new subjects there,' one of them said.

'Or else he's coming here, to get them out of the lab,' another put in.

'Two of you go to the cells,' Dr Abell snapped. 'I want someone on guard here, too, while I get to the security room to organize new search teams.'

'We'll stay here,' Jason said quickly. 'We can work on the wiring while you take care of security, Dr Abell.'

'Good. Work fast.' Dr Abell turned to the third clean-suit guy. 'You – get up to the warehouse and get me the head of security. He's up there with the outside teams. If we don't catch that kid, I'm not taking the blame by myself.'

The four of them piled out of the room, pulling off their helmets as they went. In a matter of seconds, Jason and Adam were alone with the vampires.

'Nice move,' Adam said.

'Thanks. But we have to work fast. They're all coming back.' Jason shoved his fear for Sienna down and rushed over to Zach's tank. He studied the outside, looking for a way to open it.

'Here.' Adam reached over and pushed a small button near Zach's feet. The top panel of glass slid to the side, leaving Zach open to the air. Almost immediately, the cloud of gas escaped into the room.

Jason was glad he had the clean suit on. If that gas could subdue vampires, there was no telling what it would do to humans. Quickly, Jason undid the restraints around the vampire's wrists.

'Hang on, Zach,' he said, reaching in to pull off the tape that held the tube in Zach's mouth. 'I think this might hurt.' He grabbed the tube and pulled it as smoothly as possible out of his friend's mouth. Even so, Zach began to gag, and bloody foam formed around his lips. Finally, the end of the tube appeared, and Jason sighed in relief.

'One down,' he muttered. 'You OK, man?'

Zach didn't answer.

'He's still out of it,' Jason said. 'Open the other tanks to let that gas out. It's what keeping them dazed.'

As Adam went over and opened Brad's tank, he glanced at Jason. 'That guy – Fake Me – he said he had something to keep you in line. What does that mean?'

'He's kidnapping vampires,' Jason said. 'And he's been hanging with me for two days. He knows about me and Sienna.'

Adam gasped. 'You think he's got Sienna?'

'If he does, he's a dead man,' Jason said. 'I don't care if he has vampire strength. If he hurts her—'

'Freeman,' Zach cut in. His voice was weak, but

clear. Jason spun around to see him sitting up in the tank. 'We have to get out of here.'

'You've still got an IV in.' Jason hurried over. 'Are you OK?'

Zach nodded. 'The gas is wearing off.'

Suddenly, the outer door to the lab banged open. Jason's eyes locked with Zach's. Zach dropped back down onto his back, grabbed the feeding tube, and stuffed it back into his mouth. Jason slid the restraints over his wrists without hooking them together.

Adam picked up a clipboard and went over to Van Dyke's tank. He hit the button to open it, and then began pretending to make notes as if nothing was weird. Jason turned to face the man who had just come through the sliding door of the airlock.

It was Adam. Or rather, Norton.

'Why are the tanks open?' Norton demanded, grabbing himself a gas mask from a compartment on the wall labeled 'EMERGENCY'.

'We were getting ready to wire the subjects,' Jason told him, trying to make his voice sound deeper than usual. He kept his body turned away from Norton, hoping the guy wouldn't think to look too closely. If he managed to see through the window in Jason's hood, Norton would recognize him for sure.

But Norton wasn't interested in him. He strode over to Zach's tank and leant in to see him. 'The great Zach Lafrenière,' he said tauntingly. 'Not so special now.'

Zach ignored him, gazing at the ceiling like he was still out of it.

'I hear yours is one of the purest bloodlines,' Norton went on. 'Just imagine how rich I'm going to get, thanks to your DNA.'

Jason studied Norton as he spoke. The guy didn't look so much like Adam anymore. His nose seemed bigger, and he had heavy jowls instead of Adam's thin face.

The drug is wearing off, Jason realized. *His vampire powers are weakening.*

'I'll make millions of dollars – billions, even,' Norton was saying. 'Just for spilling your secret to the world. Don't worry, Zach, you'll be a part of it. Well, your body will, anyway. Of course, I can't say for sure whether you'll survive long enough to see humans everywhere using your powers . . .'

If his appearance is slipping, then maybe his super-strength is slipping, too, Jason thought. *He's alone in the lab. Now's my chance. Maybe I can take him.*

He inched closer to Norton, working his way around the tank so he could reach the guy.

'Tell you what, I'll show you what it's like,' Norton

said, still taunting Zach. He reached into his pocket and pulled out a bottle. He popped the top, opened his mouth, and shook two red pills onto his tongue.

Those are the same as the pills from the van, Jason realized.

Before Jason could move, Norton began to transform. His nose shrunk. The jowls disappeared. The muscles of his face contracted until he was a carbon copy of Adam once again. 'This is a neat trick,' Norton told Zach. 'I don't know why you vampires don't use it more often. With different faces, you could get away with so much! Whatever you wanted to do, you could do. When this is all over, maybe I'll make myself look like you for a while. Might be a good way to lure your parents in to the lab.'

Jason saw a flicker of anger in Zach's eyes. He hoped his friend would be able to hold it together and not reveal that he was free. Norton's vampire skills were obviously back on. There was no chance Jason could beat him in a fight now. If the security guards at the warehouse were anything to go by, right now Jason would have a better chance taking on Floyd Mayweather and Oscar De La Hoya simultaneously than he would Norton after a dose of vampire-ness.

Still, Zach wasn't entirely restrained anymore. Maybe Jason could attack Norton and Zach could help.

But it was risky. He had no idea how weak Zach still was from the gas.

'Mr Norton!' a voice blared from the walkie-talkie strapped to Norton's belt. 'Are you there, sir?'

'Yes.' Norton turned away from Zach and spoke into the walkie. 'Is the complex shut down?'

'Yes, sir. We're on lockdown,' replied the unmistakable voice of the New Yorker. 'But our guest is here, and Dr Abell told her you were in the lab. She's on the way to you now, sir. And she's angry.'

'Dammit!' Norton barked. 'Send security to this lab, now.'

The outer door opened, and a tall figure strode over to the airlock. When the glass door slid back, Jason thought he might be hallucinating from all the gas. He had to be.

Because striding through the doorway, looking as glamorous – and as dangerous – as ever, was his Aunt Bianca.

Seventeen

Jason gaped at his aunt in astonishment. What on earth was she doing here?

Bianca's eyes flashed with anger, and she stalked over to Norton without even bothering to reach for a gas mask. 'What is the meaning of this?' she yelled, getting right in his face. 'How *dare* you use these vampires in your experiments!' She gestured around to the incubator tanks, specifically Zach's. 'That is a Lafrenière, for God's sake. I specifically told you he was off limits. In fact I told you *none* of these kids was to be used for experimentation. Release them this instant!'

Norton had backed off when Bianca first walked in, but now that she was screaming at him, he straightened up and advanced on her. 'I'm not releasing them now or ever,' he snapped. 'And you'd better start watching your tongue if you know what's good for you.'

Jason felt Zach's eyes on him, and Adam's. But he couldn't tear his gaze away from his aunt. He hadn't seen her since she'd tried to get Dani's ex-boyfriend to transform Dani into a vampire. His aunt was going insane as a result of her own transformation years ago, and in his mind Jason had pictured her getting smaller and thinner and, well, less powerful. But Bianca seemed as tall and strong as ever, her long dark hair cascading around her face and her deep-blue eyes practically glowing with fury.

'You little ingrate!' she growled, not backing off an inch as Norton approached. 'You'd still be languishing in some stupid think-tank if not for me.'

'Well, I'm not,' Norton sneered. 'And I'm through taking orders from you, Bianca. If you want a cure for your transformation sickness, you'd better learn to shut up and start doing as you're told.'

The outer door banged open and two big security guards appeared, armed with crossbows.

Bianca's eyes widened in surprise. 'I'll have you replaced in a heartbeat, Norton,' she snapped.

'Don't you get it? You have no power anymore,' Norton taunted her. 'You already gave me all your information — about vampires, about the purest bloodlines and where to find them. Your knowledge was your only value to me. And now that I have it, you're of no further use.'

Jason saw his aunt's shoulders began to sag a little.

He got the feeling that she hadn't realized any of that until now.

'In fact, if you weren't tainted by your disease, I would stick you in a tank and harvest *your* blood, too,' Norton said.

'We had a deal,' Bianca cried. 'I gave you that information in return for a cure. It was a *deal*!'

'Sure it was.' Norton chuckled. 'And now I'm changing the terms of the deal. So keep this in mind: if I decide to devote any of HemoCorp's resources to finding a cure for you, it will be because I want to, not because I have to.'

Bianca gathered herself and lifted her head. 'Those little pills are making you pretty brave, Norton,' she said. 'But my husband gave me some of the oldest and strongest vampire blood in existence when he transformed me. I'm one of the most powerful vampires you'll ever meet. I could snap you like a twig – right now!'

Norton chuckled and lazily gestured to the security guards at the door. One of them lowered his crossbow, taking aim at Bianca. 'Bianca, you really need to calm down,' Norton said reasonably. 'You know your transformation sickness makes you . . . unstable.'

'How dare you—' Bianca began.

'And besides, your nephew wouldn't live very long if

you snapped me like a twig,' Norton continued. 'Or didn't you know that Jason broke in here along with these three?' He gestured to Zach, Brad, and Van Dyke.

'Jason?' All at once, Bianca's bravado vanished and she actually seemed to shrink in front of Jason's eyes.

'He's in the complex. It's only a matter of time until we find him,' Norton said. 'If you want him to get out of here alive, you'll stop getting in my way.' He gestured to his men, and they stepped forward, placing themselves on either side of Bianca.

'Where are we going?' Bianca asked quietly.

'To the security center. I'm sure you'd like to watch as we take down your nephew.' Norton glanced over his shoulder at Jason and Adam. 'You two, get those vampires wired. I'll be back.'

Jason was too stunned to speak.

'Yes, sir, Mr Norton,' Adam called, his voice squeaking.

The airlock door slid closed behind Norton and Bianca, and a second later the outer door closed too. They were alone again.

'Jason—' Adam started.

'We've got to move,' Jason cut him off. He turned to Zach and found him already sitting back up, spitting out the feeding tube he'd shoved in his mouth. Zach flicked off the wrist restraints and started working on his ankle straps.

'You need help with that IV?' Jason asked.

'No,' Zach grunted. He grabbed the IV needle and jerked it out of his arm with a grimace. 'I'm good.'

Jason rushed over to Brad's tank, while Adam went to Van Dyke. Both vampires were awake. Jason untaped the tube from Brad's mouth and prepared to pull it out. 'Sorry,' he muttered, then he pulled.

Brad coughed and retched as the tube came out. 'Man, that sucked,' he finally sputtered.

'How long have you been conscious?' Jason asked.

'Long enough to watch Turnball turn into somebody else and back,' Brad muttered.

'We weren't really *un*conscious,' Zach explained, climbing out of his tank. 'Just zonked by that gas. As soon as you released it, the effects began to wear off.'

'Yeah. I heard everything that was happening,' Brad agreed, yanking out his IV as soon as Jason freed his wrists. 'By the time your aunt got here, I was just pretending to be woozy.'

'What the hell, dudes?' Van Dyke said, climbing from his tank with Adam's help. 'What's Bianca doing in league with that guy?'

'She's lost her mind,' Zach said grimly. 'There's no telling what she might do. But I have to say, I never thought she'd turn on other vampires.'

'Me neither,' Jason said sadly. 'I guess she thought Norton could help her overcome the madness.'

'Christopher!' Van Dyke cried, peering into the last incubator tank. 'Is he alive?'

'I don't know,' Jason said. 'But they didn't have the tank closed, so he's not being gassed anymore.'

Van Dyke reached in and pulled out Christopher's IV. 'Maybe it's just some kind of drug,' he said. 'They talked about putting us in comas.' He pulled out the feeding tube, then began yanking all the other tubes out of Christopher's body.

'Hey, go easy,' Jason said.

'No time,' Van Dyke grunted. 'We've got to get him out of here. He'll heal himself.'

'How do we get out?' Zach asked. 'Obviously the warehouse exit is being watched.'

'Yeah, but I've got a plan,' Jason said.

'You do?' Adam asked in surprise.

'Yup. Let's go.' Jason opened the sliding glass door and stepped into the airlock, pulling off the clean-suit helmet. Adam followed him.

'Turnball,' Brad said. 'That is the real you, right?'

'I certainly hope so,' Adam replied.

'Well, what are you doing here?' Brad asked.

'Long story,' Adam told him. 'And thanks for not

noticing that Evil McNasty was impersonating me for two days.'

'That's definitely the real Adam,' Brad said happily.

'He's awake!' Van Dyke suddenly called from the lab. He held Christopher under the arms and helped him sit up. 'You hurt, man?'

'I'll live,' Christopher croaked.

Jason couldn't believe it. The dude looked pale and weak and generally awful, but the fact that he was even conscious and talking was astonishing, given the state he'd been in just two minutes before.

'Is there anyone else in the cells?' Zach asked him. 'Any other prisoners?'

'Just some funny guy who was next to me,' Christopher said.

'That was me,' Adam told him.

'Then there's nobody else. Dr Abell told me I'd lived twice as long as any of the other vampires he worked on.' Christopher grimaced as Van Dyke helped him climb out of the tank. 'I think it's gonna take me a while to recover from this.'

'So what's the plan?' Zach asked Jason.

'Yeah, because Norton will be back any minute, and the guys who went to check on the prisoner cells are going to notice that I'm gone pretty soon,' Adam said. 'Any minute now, a bunch of guards are going to come rushing in here like Storm Troopers – and by the look of this place, they might even *have* Storm Troopers!'

'Well, good, because my plan is basically from *Star Wars*,' Jason replied. 'Adam, you and I are going to act like bad guys escorting our vampire prisoners to another part of the complex.'

'Nice. Episode Four, Han and Luke pretend Chewie's their prisoner,' Adam said.

'You two better have an *actual* plan,' Brad cut in.

'Look, we've all seen Norton, right?' Jason said. 'He looks like Adam.'

'Yeah. We get that,' Van Dyke replied. 'So?'

'So if he looks like Adam, Adam looks like him,' Jason said.

'Genius.' Zach nodded. 'Adam can pose as Norton and all the jerks who work here will listen to him because they'll think he's their boss.'

'Right. But I need some kind of disguise,' Jason said. 'I can't go walking all over in a clean suit. Adam, you have to lure a guard in here.'

'No problem. I bet this place is crawling with security right now.' Adam strode over to the door, pulled it open, and stepped out into the hallway, holding the door with one hand. 'You!' he yelled. 'I've got Jason Freeman in here. Call off the search, then get in here and help me.'

He stepped back inside, letting the door close.

'Did he buy it?' Jason asked.

'I don't know. I figured Norton's not the kind of guy who waits around to see if people are obeying him,' Adam said. 'If he shows up, we'll know he bought it.'

Two seconds later, the door opened and a security guard stepped in. 'I've cancelled the alert, Mr Norton. Where is . . . ?' his voice trailed off when he saw Jason and the vampires standing in front of him.

'I'm right here,' Jason said, flattening the guy with a punch to the jaw.

The dude jumped right back up, aiming his weapon at Jason, but Brad was too fast for him. He grabbed the crossbow out of the guy's hand and turned it until the point of the bolt was at his throat.

The guard froze, and Zach and Van Dyke grabbed his arms. Jason was about to clock him again, when someone got there before him.

Christopher.

The injured vampire had found a surge of desperate energy from somewhere, and had latched onto the guard like a leech, his teeth going straight for the man's neck.

Jason hesitated a moment, reminding himself that Christopher needed the boost, however tough it was to watch. After the vampire had taken four or five loud gulps, Jason shot Zach a look.

Zach nodded back as he prised Christopher off the guard, who had that blissful, drunken look of a human who had just been fed on.

'That's enough,' Zach told him. 'We have to get moving.'

'I need his uniform,' Jason said.

'You heard him,' Adam told the guard. 'Strip.'

The guard was so out of it, he obeyed Adam's command without complaint. When the guy had taken off his dark-blue jacket and pants, Brad and Zach dragged him over to the incubator tanks and made him climb inside. They taped his mouth shut with the medical tape and tied his hands and feet with the restraints.

Jason took off the clean suit and put on the guard's uniform. 'Let's go,' he said.

'You need the crossbow,' Zach said, handing it to him.

Jason took it reluctantly. He'd been shot with a crossbow. He didn't really want to touch one, ever. But Zach was right. He needed it to look like a real guard.

'Everybody look beat,' Jason instructed the vampires. 'As if you're prisoners and you're totally unable to escape from us.'

'No problem,' Christopher said, leaning on Van Dyke for support. Though he was looking a little stronger, he was still a long way off full strength. But then, he wasn't a Malibu vampire.

'They have motorized supply carts,' Jason remembered. 'If we pass one, our fake Mr Norton can commandeer it to carry the disabled prisoner.'

'Will do,' Adam promised.

Just as Jason reached for the door handle, something vibrated against his side. He jumped, startled. It took him a moment to realize it was his cell phone. He'd been so consumed by events down here in the complex that he'd practically forgotten about the world outside.

He pulled out the phone and checked the ID. 'It's Sienna,' he told the others, hitting the 'Talk' button. 'Are you OK?' he asked her.

'Yes. Are you?' The sound of her husky voice instantly made him feel better.

'We're having some trouble. This thing is bigger than we realized,' he told her.

'I know. Jason, the DeVere lab analyzed those red pills. You won't believe it—'

'They give humans vampire strength and vampire powers,' Jason said. 'I know. I've seen them in action.'

'Oh.' Sienna sounded confused.

'They work really well,' Jason told her. 'They let the

head of this operation shape shift to look like Adam. He set us all up.'

'*What?*' Sienna cried.

'Don't worry, the real Adam is here,' Jason assured her, smiling at Adam as he spoke. But Adam wasn't looking at him. He was staring at something on the inside of the door. Staring intently.

'Hang on,' Jason told Sienna. 'What's up, Adam?'

'This is a floor plan. Evacuation routes and alarm system status and all that,' Adam said. 'Look at it.'

Jason did. Zach looked over his shoulder. The thing was like a big computerized map of the complex, with temperature readings, blinking lights to indicate working alarms, and information readouts on laboratory conditions in all the rooms.

'This lab must be the nerve center,' Zach said. 'From here, you can see what's going on everywhere else and keep track of all the experiments.'

'Which is pretty damn cool,' Adam said. 'But that's not what I'm interested in. Look. This is the warehouse,' Adam pointed to it on the floor plan, 'so these must be the hallways we're in right now. They're like tunnels that burrow under the hill.'

Jason nodded.

'This place is huge,' Zach said. 'These tunnels – hallways, whatever – seem to go on forever.'

'No, they have an end,' Adam replied. 'Right here, in this building.' He pointed to one end of the floor plan, as far from their location as could be.

Jason frowned. 'A building? But the warehouse was in the middle of nowhere.'

'The tunnels go on for miles,' Zach said. 'And they go under the hills. That building, on the outside, is nowhere near the warehouse. They're just connected underground.'

'Connected *secretly*,' Adam added.

'Where is that building?' Zach asked.

But Jason had a sick feeling that he already knew the answer. 'It's on Mulholland Highway,' he said quietly. 'It's the headquarters of Medi-Life.'

Eighteen

'Oh, my God,' Adam said. 'You're right.'

'Oh, my God,' Sienna simultaneously gasped over the phone. 'Medi-Life?'

'They're behind this whole thing,' Jason told her. 'Remember the HemoCorp pen you found? Well, their logo is all over the place here. And HemoCorp is owned by Medi-Life.'

'Jason,' Sienna said. 'This is really, really bad.'

'I know. They've got so much money that this place is rigged like a maximum-security prison. It's going to be hard to get out,' Jason said.

'No, I mean it's bad because of the red pills,' Sienna explained. 'If it's Medi-Life developing this drug ... well, it means they're planning to distribute it somehow. I bet the military would pay big bucks for a pill that turned regular people into super-soldiers.'

'Not to mention what people would pay on the black market,' Jason muttered. 'Mr Norton, the big cheese, is already talking about the billions of dollars he's going to make.'

'That's not the worst of it,' Sienna went on. 'The DeVere researchers said the pills are unstable. The formula breaks down unpredictably, and the side effects on any humans taking them could be fatal.'

'Well, I wish they were fatal sooner,' Jason said. 'I'd really like it if Norton toppled over right about now.'

'Jason, you guys have to get out of there,' Sienna said.

'I'm on it!' Jason replied, then a thought struck him. 'I wonder if they're storing the drug here or someplace else . . .'

'What's going on?' Zach demanded.

Jason quickly filled him in on Sienna's discovery. 'Even if we get out of here alive, we'll be leaving these goons with stockpiles of a dangerous drug,' Jason concluded.

'But if we could get rid of it, we'd be setting their research back by months!' Adam put in.

Jason turned to Christopher. 'Did you hear anything about the pills? Where they might be keeping them?'

'No. Sorry.' Christopher shook his head.

'Jason,' Sienna said. 'The researchers here say it's easy to destroy the drug . . .'

'Excellent! But, how?' Jason asked.

He heard Sienna talking to someone on her end of the phone. 'They say it's very delicate,' she finally told him. 'The active ingredient needs to be kept at around room temperature. If you can expose the pills to warm temperatures, the active ingredient will break down, and the drugs will be ruined.'

'OK, so we just have to turn up the heat,' Jason said. 'But I still don't know how to find it.'

'I do,' Adam put in.

Jason looked at his best friend quizzically.

'Temperature readings.' Adam pointed to the computerized floor plan.

'Yes! Find someplace that's cold,' Jason told him. 'And that looks big enough to store a bunch of medicine.'

'Belle and I are going to head over to the warehouse right now,' Sienna said. 'It sounds like you guys need help.'

'No!' Jason cried. He turned away while Adam and Zach studied the floor plan. 'Don't go to the warehouse. They'll be waiting for you and they'll grab you both.'

'OK, then, where should we meet you?'

Jason thought about it. 'At the Medi-Life headquarters. This whole place is a big, secret lab. I doubt the regular people who work in the Medi-Life building know anything about it. So if we can get there, we might be able to get out. Can Belle's car take all of us?'

'Yeah, we took her parents' Escalade,' Sienna said, confusion in her voice. 'But I don't understand. You're just going to walk out the front door?'

'If the plan works, yes. A very public exit could be our only chance.' Jason took a deep breath. 'Be careful. I love you.'

'You too.' Sienna's voice shook a little. 'I'll see you soon.'

'Let's hope so,' Jason muttered as he stuck his phone back in his pocket.

'We got it,' Adam reported. 'There's a room two hallways from here. It's the only room on the whole corridor, and the temperature is a steady thirty degrees.'

'Refrigerated.' Jason grinned. 'Is it on our way to the Medi-Life building?'

'Yup.' Adam pulled open the door. 'Let's go.'

The hallway was empty when they stepped out, but Jason could hear voices calling to one another from somewhere nearby. 'This way – fast.' He gestured to the right, where the hall intersected another hall.

But the vampires couldn't go very fast. Christopher had to be supported by both Van Dyke and Brad in order to even walk.

'We need to find carts,' Jason told Adam.

'I'm on it.' Adam turned onto the next hall and spotted a maintenance man. 'You!' he yelled. 'Two carts, pronto. I need them for the prisoners.'

The maintenance guy jumped, then turned and raced down the hall. 'Right away, Mr Norton!' he called over his shoulder.

'Stay here and wait for the carts,' Jason told his friends. 'I'm going to find that storage room and turn up the heat.'

He jogged away from the group and turned back onto the original hallway. The room they'd seen on the floor plan was two corridors up. Jason slowed as he passed a man in a lab suit rushing the other way, then sped up again until he reached the second corridor.

This place was deserted. The corridor was short, a dead end. And sure enough, there was only one door. Jason pulled Bill Baldwin's ID out of his pocket. 'Tell me you had drug access, Bill,' he whispered. Holding his breath, he swiped the card. The door clicked open.

A rush of relief flooded Jason, and he smiled. Inside, the room was cold and dark, and Jason could sense that it was a big place. Luckily, the temperature controls were right inside the doorway, protected by a plastic covering.

'Finally, something that's easy,' Jason murmured. He

smashed the plastic with his fist, then hit the red 'Up' arrow to raise the temperature. He pushed it to the maximum: eighty degrees. Then he hit 'Enter'.

And an alarm went off.

'Damn it!' Jason looked up – red lights were flashing over the doorway, and bells were clanging through the hallway, echoing up and down the other corridors.

Jason slammed the door, then grabbed the crossbow bolt from his weapon and stabbed it into the sensor pad, scratching and tearing at it until there was no way anybody could use it to unlock the door and turn down the thermostat.

Then he ran. Back to the main corridor, down to the first intersection, and over to his friends. They had two motorized carts and were just settling Christopher onto the back of one of them.

'Something you want to tell us?' Adam asked as Jason ran up.

'Yeah. It's time to go.' Jason jumped onto the cart with Christopher and Van Dyke, spun the little wheel, and hit the gas. The thing shot off down the hall. Adam leapt behind the wheel of the second cart while Zach and Brad jumped into the back.

The maintenance man watched, baffled, as Adam sped away with a wave.

Jason reached the end of the hallway and took a

right, keeping an image of the floor plans in his mind. 'This corridor should lead us straight to the Medi-Life building,' he told the vampires, hitting the gas until they were at maximum speed.

'When?' Van Dyke asked, peering ahead. The hallway vanished into the distance, no end in sight.

'I don't know. I think it's a couple of miles,' Jason said.

He heard Adam's cart behind him, picking up speed. After a minute or two, the sounds of the alarm behind them began to fade. There were no more doors, just smooth white walls. This section was clearly just a connector to the main building, not part of the HemoCorp complex anymore.

'We might make it,' Jason said. 'This might actually work!'

Just then, two guards appeared about fifty yards ahead, standing at attention.

'Oh, no,' Adam moaned. 'A security checkpoint! Meaning, that's two guys who could potentially go Bruce Banner on our asses. Look sharp, folks.'

Jason slammed on the brakes, squealing to a stop just a few feet from the men.

Adam's cart crashed into his, pushing him further toward them.

The guards both lifted their crossbows. 'This

hallway is off limits,' one of them growled. 'Orders from Mr Norton.'

Adam jumped off his cart, walked right up to the bigger guy and swatted the crossbow out of the way. 'We've got a situation in the complex,' he said. 'Don't you hear the alarms? Get back there and check it out while I escort the test subjects to a secure area.'

The two guards stared at him for a second as the alarms blared dimly in the distance.

'Go!' Adam yelled.

They took off at a run down the long white corridor. Jason grinned at Adam, raising his eyebrows.

'I could get used to being in charge,' Adam joked, climbing back on to his cart. 'For anyone who wasn't paying attention, I was channeling James Caan from *Godfather* one, just without the hammy New York accent. But even *you* guys must have known that, right?' Adam read the look on all their faces. He sighed. 'Not the right time, I guess.'

Jason hit the gas again, and they sped on.

'I see something,' Van Dyke said a minute later.

Jason squinted into the whiteness. 'Yeah,' he agreed. There was something silver up ahead.

After another minute it became clear: silver doors. Silver *elevator* doors.

'We're here,' Adam cheered from the other cart. 'The

corridor ends at the elevators. They must lead up to the main Medi-Life building.'

They pulled the carts to a stop, and Jason jumped off and hit the 'Up' button on the elevators. The others helped Christopher off the cart, practically lifting him into the air and setting him on his feet. Jason bit his lip. The guy was in really bad shape.

Sienna and Belle are coming with a car, he thought. *Let's just hope they get here in time.*

With a soft buzz, the elevator arrived. Jason half-expected Norton to jump out of the opening doors, but nothing happened. It was just a regular elevator. They all piled in, and Jason pushed the button that said 'Lobby'.

The elevator shot up with a *whoosh* . . . and kept on going.

'How far underground are we?' Zach asked.

Adam shrugged. 'If the tunnel goes through the hills, there's no telling how deep it is. The Medi-Life building is at the top of the hill.'

Finally, the doors opened and they all stepped out into a huge marble lobby. The ceiling over the lobby was made of glass, letting in the pale light of early morning. Jason blinked, staring up at the blue California sky. Had they really been down in the HemoCorp complex all night?

'This is surreal,' Brad muttered, glancing around at the corporate lobby. Sunlight glinted off a waterfall along the back wall, the smell of fresh coffee wafted over from a fully stocked breakfast stand, and polished-looking workers were making their way in for the day.

Jason nodded. It was bizarre to come from the hi-tech, nightmarish vampire experimentation labs, up here to normality, all just by taking an elevator.

Judging from the looks they were getting, the people on their way to work found it pretty bizarre to see a bunch of exhausted teenage guys and a security guard with a crossbow, too. Jason pulled out his cell and speed-dialled Sienna.

'Where are you?' he asked when she picked up.

'About half a mile from Medi-Life,' she reported. 'We'll be there soon.'

'I need you to get to the front entrance. Just pull as close to the doors as you can,' Jason told her. 'Christopher won't be able to make it much farther than that.'

He hung up and they started across the lobby toward freedom. Jason could feel the tension melting out of his body. They were nearly out, and surely nobody would dare to stop them in a public place like this!

He glanced over at Van Dyke and Brad, supporting Christopher. 'Will he be OK?' he asked Zach.

Zach nodded. 'We'll keep him here in Malibu until he's fully healed.'

Jason looked at the bank of doors ahead, leading out to the parking lot. No sight had ever seemed so beautiful to him.

'Freeze!' yelled a deep voice. 'Stay right where you are!'

Suddenly, about eight guys with crossbows rushed the lobby, lining themselves up in front of the doors. In the center was the big New Yorker they'd fought at the warehouse. Jason and his friends stopped walking.

'You idiots,' someone said from behind them. 'Did you actually think you could escape when I have the entire place under constant surveillance?'

Jason turned to find Norton-Adam approaching them from the elevators, Bianca and Dr Abell behind him.

'You're scaring the Medi-Life employees,' Zach said smoothly. He nodded toward the scandalized people in suits who had gathered around to watch.

Norton turned to them. 'This is a security procedure drill,' he announced. 'Please go to your offices and remain there until I give further instructions.'

Murmuring in confusion, the workers all headed for

the elevators or for doors to the hallways leading off the lobby. Suddenly one of the front doors opened and a girl in a business suit rushed in, not even seeming to notice the guys with crossbows.

'Close the entrance!' Norton snapped. 'Direct new arrivals to the side door.' One of the guards rushed outside to do it.

But Jason was still watching the girl in the suit.

So was Adam. 'Brianna?' he gasped.

The girl stopped and looked up. It was definitely Brianna. Her face paled as she looked from Adam to Norton and back. But she wasn't surprised, Jason noticed. It was as if she'd known all along that there were two Adams.

'Of course!' Adam murmured. 'She set me up! She asked me to drive out to get her, and that's when I was ambushed.'

'I guess she's been working for Norton all along,' Jason said quietly.

'Take the subjects back down to the complex,' Norton ordered the guards.

Four of the guys started forward, crossbows up. Jason felt a wave of exhaustion. They'd already managed to escape so many times in the past few hours. How were they ever going to pull it off again?

Suddenly, Adam stepped in front of the guards.

'You morons!' he shouted. 'Don't listen to him. Don't you even know who you're working for? That's Adam Turnball. *I'm* Mr Norton.'

Nineteen

The guards hesitated, confused, letting their weapons drop a little.

'Do you think some *kid* would be able to make off with four vampires?' Adam asked, his voice dripping sarcasm. 'I should have you all replaced by people with brains.'

The guards looked doubtful, and one of them raised his crossbow again. But he didn't seem entirely sure which version of Adam to point it at.

'Listen to him,' Bianca cried suddenly. Jason shot a look at his aunt. She was gazing at him, a pleading expression on her face.

She's sorry, he realized. *She wants me to forgive her.* For a brief moment, she looked so much like his old, cool Aunt Bianca that a lump formed in Jason's throat. But there was no time to get emotional right now.

'*That's* Mr Norton,' Bianca said, pointing at Adam. 'He's your boss. The other one has been holding me hostage all this time. He wanted to use me as a bargaining chip to get his friends back.'

'How dare you!' Norton roared.

But Bianca's trick had worked. The guards lowered their crossbows, totally confused. They glanced back and forth between the two Nortons – or the two Adams.

'I'm sorry, sir,' said the New Yorker, addressing both of them. 'But we have no idea which is the real you.'

'I'm the real me,' Adam said, brimming with confidence now. 'Thank you for clarifying things, Bianca.' He stared the New Yorker straight in the eye. 'Now, escort the real Adam Turnball back to his cell.'

'I've had enough of this.' Norton strode forward angrily. Some of the guards aimed their weapons at him.

This is working perfectly, Jason thought, shooting his friend a grateful look. He took advantage of the guards' confusion to inch toward the doors. Zach, Brad, Van Dyke and Christopher took the hint and moved that way, too.

Norton stopped, staring aghast at his own guards pointing crossbows at him. 'The impostor is right about one thing,' he snarled. 'I should replace you all!'

'Are you calling *me* an impostor?' Adam snapped.

'Yes.' Norton turned to face him, and the two

versions of Adam glared at each other – until one of them began to change. As Jason watched, Norton's nose grew longer, his cheeks heftier. His ears went from sticking out to drooping. His eyes developed bags underneath them, and his entire body seemed to thicken. In a matter of seconds, he was a middle-aged man.

Bianca turned to Jason. 'Run!' she yelled.

Jason ran, barreling through two of the guards to open the door and hold it for his friends. Zach sped through, but Brad and Van Dyke were moving more slowly as they helped Christopher.

By the time they reached the door, the guards had all recovered from their confusion and were aiming their crossbows at the fugitives.

'No!' Norton yelled. 'We need the vampires alive. Shoot for their legs.'

A crossbow bolt flew at Brad's thigh.

Jason jumped for him, pushing him out of the way just as the metal bolt sliced through the air and hit the glass door. The door shattered, showering little cubes of safety glass across the floor.

'Run! Go! Go!' Jason yelled, pushing the four vampires ahead of him. They were all outside now.

Jason turned to find Adam. His friend had skirted the guards to the back, and he was sprinting for a door at the opposite end of the entrance from Jason.

'Jason, get out of here,' Bianca called. She was heading his way, fending off a guard who had her by the arm.

Outside, Jason heard the squeal of brakes and saw Belle's car jump the curb and skid to a stop on the sidewalk in front of the building. Brad and Van Dyke dragged Christopher toward the car.

'Aunt Bianca!' Jason called, turning back. But he'd lost sight of her in the press of guards.

'Kill the humans!' Norton commanded. 'Stop the vampires!'

The New Yorker looked right at Jason and aimed his crossbow at his chest. Jason stood for a second, paralyzed, his shoulder aching where Tamburo's crossbow bolt had almost killed him several months before.

Time seemed to slow down as the New Yorker shot his weapon.

Jason watched in sick fascination as the deadly bolt flew toward him. *It's not going to hit my shoulder this time*, he realized. *It's going to hit my heart*.

He was moving, he knew. He was diving out of the way. But it was too late. The bolt was coming for him. It was about to hit him—

And then Bianca was in front of Jason, blocking his

view of the crossbow bolt. There was a confusion of dark hair flying, a strange sound from Bianca like the air being let out of a tire, and her body slammed against his.

Then suddenly everything sped up again, and Jason was falling with Aunt Bianca on top of him. He landed on the sidewalk outside the door, and his aunt rolled to the side. A crossbow bolt was sticking out of her chest.

'Aunt Bianca!' Jason cried. He grabbed her shoulders, trying to ignore the way her head flopped to the side. 'Aunt Bianca!'

'Freeman.' Zach was at his side. 'We have to go.'

'My aunt . . .' Jason couldn't stop staring at her face. Her eyes were open, staring. Her lips were pale.

'She's gone. Leave her.' Zach pulled at his arm, but Jason shoved him away.

'Jason.' Now Adam was there, too. 'We have to go. Right now. Come on!'

Jason glanced up at his best friend. Adam's eyes looked haunted, but his face was determined.

'I can't just leave her.' But Jason was up and moving; somehow he was running, with Adam holding one arm and Zach holding the other.

In front of them, Belle's car door was open. Van Dyke and Christopher were already in the far back row. Zach shoved Jason in, and Brad pulled him across the seat so Adam and Zach could climb in behind him.

Belle peeled out, the door still open. Jason saw guards running after them, crossbows aimed. A loud, metallic *thunk* made the car shake as they bounced down off the curb and took off into the parking lot.

'I think they shot your parents' car,' Van Dyke said.

'We have insurance,' Belle muttered, hitting the gas.

In the passenger seat, Sienna turned to look at the guys, her eyes roving over all of them, and stopping on Jason.

'Everybody OK?' she asked.

Her dark eyes seemed to pour comfort into his soul, and, for the first time in hours, Jason felt safe. He nodded, as Adam gave a faint smile.

'Yeah,' Adam said. 'I can't quite believe it, but I think we're all going to live.'

Twenty

'Fireworks!' Sienna declared four days later.

Jason looked at his girlfriend in her strapless minidress and nodded. 'I'll say.' He grabbed her around the waist and pulled her down to sit on his lap on the couch.

Sienna laughed and smacked him lightly on the arm. 'No, I mean actual fireworks. Zach says they're starting in five minutes. He got a professional firm to do them, so they should be spectacular.'

'Figures.' Jason laughed, gesturing around Zach's incredible house, which was filled with about a hundred people at the moment, all of them laughing, dancing, drinking and generally having the best time of their entire lives. Graduation had been yesterday, and Zach was having the party of the century to celebrate. 'Everything here is spectacular.'

Jason spotted Danielle dancing with her friends Kristy and Billy under a gigantic disco ball that had been hung in the living room. Van Dyke and Maggie were cuddled up on a *chaise longue* in front of the ten-foot-wide fireplace, complete with roaring fire. Adam was interviewing Brad on camera, and Erin and Belle were busy flirting with a couple of senior guys from school.

Graduates, Jason corrected himself. *None of us are seniors anymore. We're high-school graduates.*

It felt strange to even think the words. Jason wondered if he'd ever get used to the feeling. He sighed. Graduation had been bittersweet, so soon after losing his aunt.

'Thinking about Bianca?' Sienna asked, taking his hand.

'You're too good at reading me,' Jason told her with a smile. 'I know I shouldn't be thinking about Aunt Bianca at a party. I should be enjoying myself, happy to be with my friends one last time before we all scatter to our colleges.'

Sienna squeezed his hand. 'It's all right to feel sad, even at a party. Bianca was family and you loved her.'

'She sacrificed herself to save me,' Jason said. 'I still can't believe she did that.'

'She loved you, too,' Sienna told him. 'But, Jason, it's really a gift that she died that way. The transformation sickness was killing her. She was facing a long, slow, agonizing death. At least, this way, she's out of her misery. And she did a noble thing and saved you.' Sienna leant closer and trailed her fingers along his cheek. 'I know I'll be grateful to her forever for that.'

Jason kissed her, letting his lips linger on hers for a moment.

'Fireworks,' Zach announced from the balcony.

'I'll say,' Sienna joked, looking up at Jason.

He grinned, then followed Zach and Sienna out to the balcony.

'Worth filming? I think not,' Adam said, coming up beside Jason and Sienna on the big balcony overlooking the Pacific.

'I didn't think there was anything you found unworthy of filming,' Jason said, surprised.

'My friend, look at those fireworks. They are spectacular. No camera could capture their true beauty.' Adam sighed dreamily as the first round of fireworks exploded over the water, sending a thousand stars raining down from the sky while their reflections shot up from the depths of the ocean. 'Unless, you know, I had a really big special effects budget,' Adam added.

As the fireworks continued with everyone gasping at each new explosion, Jason felt a hand on his shoulder. Zach drew him away from the crowd.

'Freeman, I wanted you to know there was a DeVere Heights Vampire Council meeting this afternoon,' he said quietly. 'We got the help of the High Council on this one, and we've managed to recover Bianca's body from the Medi-Life building. I know your mother will want to give her a proper funeral.'

'Yes,' Jason said. 'Thank you.'

'Also, we're going to take care of everything,' Zach went on. 'We don't want you or your parents to have to deal with any of it. The official police report will list Bianca's death as a result of experimental drug testing done by Medi-Life. We've had the entire complex searched, and we've exposed some of the facts to the media, enough to make life very uncomfortable for Charles Norton. In fact, HemoCorp has already been disbanded and we've begun a wrongful death lawsuit against Medi-Life.'

'So it's over?' Jason asked. 'We don't have to worry about them anymore?'

'Believe me, we'll litigate Medi-Life into non-existence,' Zach said. 'That's the kind of thing the Vampire High Council does best.'

'I appreciate it,' Jason told him. 'I'm glad I'll have something to tell my mom.'

Zach nodded. 'Christopher's heading back to New York in the morning. He's going to tell the Vampire Council there how Bianca really died – with honor. It will go a long way toward restoring her legacy.'

Jason had got a glimpse of Christopher earlier. He'd come down to the party for a half hour or so before heading back upstairs to bed.

'Christopher's really OK, huh? He looked good when I saw him before.' Jason smiled. 'Only four days of healing – pretty impressive.'

'Well, he *is* a vampire,' Zach said.

Jason raised an eyebrow at the haughty tone in Zach's voice, but then he noticed the smile playing around his friend's mouth.

'How could I forget?' Jason murmured with a grin, as Zach walked away.

When Jason returned to Sienna and Adam, he found his best friend complaining loudly over the booming of the fireworks. 'I'm doomed. Just doomed to be single forever. How can I ever trust a girl again?' he was saying. 'The way Brianna set me up ... She was like Kathleen Turner in *Body Heat.*'

'Wow, really? Your girlfriend asked you to kill her husband for her? That's hardcore!' a girl standing nearby exclaimed.

Adam whirled around to look at her. She was short and cute, with a dark-red pixie haircut and a T-shirt with a picture of Snoopy on it.

'You don't go to DeVere High,' Adam said.

'Nope,' she replied.

'You've actually seen *Body Heat*,' he went on.

'Sure. It's an incredible movie,' she replied.

'Who directed it?' Adam asked.

'What is this, a quiz?' the girl demanded.

'Yes.' Adam tried to look stern, and Jason had to turn away to hide his smile. Sienna pressed her head against his shoulder to muffle her giggles.

'Lawrence Kasdan,' the girl said. 'Duh.'

'I think I love you,' Adam replied. 'Want to go inside and get a drink?'

As they headed for the swanky bar set up in Zach's kitchen, Jason and Sienna burst out laughing. 'So much for Adam being doomed to singlehood,' she said.

The fireworks had ended, and everybody was drifting back to the party. But Jason found himself wanting to stay out here, with the roar of the surf in his ears, and Sienna in his arms.

Maggie and Van Dyke stood nearby, gazing out at the ocean. And Brad, Erin and Belle had perched themselves on the stone wall surrounding the balcony. It seemed that nobody else wanted to leave, either. Jason smiled. Here he was, hanging out with a bunch of vampires.

How was he ever going to go back to having a normal social life after this?

Zach appeared from inside, a bottle of champagne

in his hand. He looked around at the group and raised the bottle. 'A toast to surviving our senior year,' he said. He grinned at Jason. 'With a little help from our friends.'

The vampires all applauded. Zach handed the bottle to Jason, and Jason held it up. 'And one more toast . . . to friendship.'

'That was a great party,' Sienna said a few hours later, resting her head against the back of the VW's passenger seat.

'As always,' Jason agreed.

'I think it was better than usual,' Sienna said. 'Maybe because it was the last one.'

The VW gave a loud groan and sputtered to a stop in the middle of the road. 'What the hell?' Jason said. He turned the key – nothing. The car was totally dead.

Sienna burst out laughing. 'Now you know what it's like! You'll never be able to make fun of my car again!'

'I will too,' Jason muttered.

He tried the car two more times, but it was no good.

'We can just walk home from here. It's less than a mile,' Sienna pointed out.

'I can't leave the car in the middle of the street.'

'We'll push it to the side,' Sienna said. 'I do have super-strength, you know. I could push this thing one-handed.'

'You trying to intimidate me?' Jason teased, as they got out and pushed the car to the curb.

'Is it working?' Sienna teased back. 'Some guys like a girl who's a little intimidating.'

Jason put on his best 'hick from Michigan' expression. 'Well, I don't know how you Malibu girls flirt, but us boys from the flyovers like to say what they mean.'

'And what *do* you mean?' Sienna asked, stepping closer to him.

Jason breathed in the incredible scent of her. 'I mean I love you, super-strength and all,' he murmured.

'And I love you.' Sienna brushed her lips against his. 'You know, my parents are off visiting Paige this weekend. The house is empty.'

'An empty house,' Jason mused. 'And no vampire crisis happening to distract us. I wasn't sure that would ever happen.'

'Some things are worth waiting for,' Sienna told him.

And Sienna is one of them, Jason thought, watching her walk on down the dark street, her long hair gleaming in the starlight.

'Are you coming?' she called.

'Oh, yeah,' he said, jogging after her. 'Wherever you're going, Sienna Devereux, I'm going too.'

Secrets at St Jude's

New Girl

By Carmen Reid

Ohmigod! Gina's mum has finally flipped and is sending her to Scotland to some crusty old *boarding school* called St Jude's – just because Gina spent all her money on clothes and got a few bad grades! It's so *unfair!*

Now the Californian mall-rat has to swap her sophisticated life of pool parties and well-groomed boys for . . . hockey *in the rain*, school dinners and stuffy housemistresses. And what's with her three kooky dorm-buddies . . . could they ever be her *friends?* And just how does a St Jude's girl get out to meet the gorgeous guys invited to the school's summer ball?

978 0 552 55706 1

www.rbooks.co.uk

Antonio Pagliarulo

The Hamilton triplets – Madison, Park and Lexington – are accustomed to living in the public eye. Heiresses to a billion-dollar media empire, they have been raised in New York's most elite social circles and, at sixteen, know first hand the demands of being celebutantes. It isn't always about designer labels and lavish parties. There are people to impress, appearances to make, and paparazzi to outrun. Not to mention high school to finish.

But when fashion editor Zahara Bell is found dead in a one-of-a-kind frock from Lex's unreleased clothing line, and then the priceless Avenue diamond goes missing, getting to class is as far from the triplets' minds as their first pair of Manolos. One of the girls is a suspect, and the sisters find themselves in the middle of a scandal that could sink their reputations and their father's companies for good. And the press is ready, willing and able to lend a hand.

The Hamilton sisters need to stick closer together than ever before – the killer is still out there, and if they don't solve the case, their (sometimes) good name could become dirtier than a certain hotel chain. And their threesome could turn into a twosome quicker than you can say Cartier . . .

ISBN: 978 1 862 30462 8